MERRY LITTLE MYSTIC MURDER

Book One: Phoebe Monday
Paranormal Cozies

PATTI LARSEN

Copyright © 2020 Patti Larsen
All rights reserved.

Thanks, Kirstin!

ISBN-13: 978-1-989925-41-6

CHAPTER ONE

Do you have any idea how hard it is to focus on spell casting with Jingle Bells running in your head?

Hard. Trust me.

Still, this was my favorite part, despite the subject and content, endless chatter pulling my focus, scent of pumpkin spice and pine dominating the air in the bullpen. Maybe that meant something about me, how enjoying the process of uncovering things people thought hidden brought me joy and peace, far more than carols or the holiday season or eggnog lattes.

And maybe it just meant I was good at what I did.

I focused on the way the pencil felt in my hand, the weight of my sketchbook perched on my knee, the rhythm and tone of the old man's voice as he spoke past the endlessly irritating Christmas songs playing at someone's desk. Allowed the power within me to block out the sounds of the police department, how my stomach growled for a gingerbread cookie I spotted on the way in, into the words the elderly homeless Unk Jay-Jay used to describe his attacker.

I always compare the beginning to blowing a bubble, the skin of the surface of the spell shining, catching light as though created from the sparkling edge of a rainbow, moving in a slow dance across the surface as it grew and enveloped first the speaker, then drew me inside, washing across me in the gentlest sigh of welcome.

The. Best. Part.

Being inside someone else's experience had its downfalls, especially in cases like this. Witnessing the attack he'd undergone the night before, seeing the source of the bruise on his left cheek, certainly had nothing pleasant about it. And yet, there was this delicious connection, a deeply abiding contentment to sharing in the moment I would never, ever take for granted.

And, of course, once I was in, I had control of the memory, so I didn't have to live through the pain of the blow that carried poor Unk to the ground. Instead, I stepped into that instant in time, and took a look around.

The dark alley's only illumination came from a streetlight at the far end, just enough whitewash cast to throw shadows and highlight bits and pieces of the scene. I stepped around Unk and the rusting shopping car piled high with the possessions he deemed worthy, skimming across a puddle of something oozing from the bottom of a dented dumpster. There were faint, warbled sounds in the frozen moment, distorted by the stillness of time, a scent that translated from his experience to mine, though not a breath of air. I could even vaguely taste from his perspective, though I tried not to focus on such details. I wasn't here to be him. I was here to know what he knew, even if he couldn't remember.

The mind endlessly fascinated me, knowing how much we absorbed while only consciously registering a fraction of the massive amount of information available at any given moment. Sucked when someone tried to recall, but worked well with my particular little talent.

Normal people had no idea how powerful words could be. But I knew.

The attacker wasn't big, though he had at least four inches or so on me. Mind you, I wasn't what you'd call tall myself, barely the five-foot-one I claimed on my driver's license. I had the immediate impression of youth from the image, of a slender body inside that dark hoody and jeans, sneakers new enough but unremarkable in their branding. Of course he wore a ski mask, disguising his features. Sometimes I could see past the thick weave of cloth, but only if the victim had personal contact with their attacker, subliminal cues missed in the moment but easily uncovered when I stepped into their memory. This time, it was clear to me either Unk had no previous contact with the young man who'd struck him down and stolen from his cart or any such possible interaction was, instead, casual and momentary enough it didn't stick in Unk's head.

I sighed over the lack of detail, the light not sufficient to identify eye color, though they did appear dark to me, the lashes long and thick enough most girls would envy them. The lips had a unique shape at least, a small scar marring the right side of the cupid's bow, tugging it slightly askew. A detail that could help in the long run.

Circling the memory didn't help much, Unk's lack of information meant there was only darkness when I tried to look behind the young man, the solid line between what he'd seen and what he hadn't an endless source of frustration.

"How's it going over here?"

I jerked in surprise, crying out a little, dropping my pencil. The return to the bullpen hit me in a blow of disorienting reality, sights and sounds washing away the crystal clear moment I'd been lost in. Part of me hated coming back to the real world. The quiet and stillness of memory had such an anchoring sensation, being forced to return meant a solid ten seconds of blinking and being the weirdo I knew I was in plain view of everyone.

Officer Cooper Hudson was already bending to retrieve my pencil, his tall, muscular self brushing against my left knee, the scent of the delicious but subtle cologne he wore another layer of reality that helped bring me back despite myself. His apologetic grin with those perfect white teeth and the utter focus in his pale green eyes always made me blush for some reason.

Maybe because I wasn't used to being the center

of anyone's attention. Not with the family I came from.

"Sorry, Phoebe," Coop said in that lovely bass voice of his, handing me my pencil, the tip broken from its contact with the tile floor. He hesitated, noticing at the same moment I did, regret surfacing on his expressive face. One thing about Coop, I never had to wonder what he was feeling. A heart that big had trouble disguising itself.

"It's fine." I took the pencil, tucking it under the flap of my satchel. "I think we're done anyway." It was the first time since exploring his memory I looked up and met Unk's eyes and found him grinning past his heavy silver beard, his sharp, blue gaze flickering back and forth between me and Coop fast enough I knew what he was thinking.

Which made me blush all over again.

"You two make a cute couple," Unk said before hiccupping. The faint scent of alcohol reached me, his red nose lined with broken capillaries and the shaking of his hands clear indication he'd be seeking another drink or many the moment I was done with him.

I looked down at the sketchbook in my lap, the image I'd drawn with my body while my spirit had been lost in the bubble of his memory. Turned the book around to show Unk who nodded with enthusiasm before sighing another aromatic breath.

"That's him," Unk said. "That's the creep." His pale eyes brimmed with tears, snuffle following, one dirty gloved hand rising to swipe over the tip of that bulbous red nose. As though the fabled Santa Claus had somehow fallen on hard times. "Didn't see his face, like I told the detectives."

I smiled my encouragement. "You did great, Unk," I said, while Coop whistled at the image.

"No wonder you're our favorite sketch artist," he said. Blushed himself. Leaned back and cleared his throat, arms crossing over his uniform shirt. "Nice work, Miss Monday."

"Officer Hudson." He perked instantly at the sound of his name, left in a rush but making sure to take a moment to smile at me with that glowingly optimistic mindset of his making him practically shimmer to someone like me. I couldn't help but watch him stride off to the other side of the bullpen, though I swear it was his aura that held my attention.

Not looking at his well-formed and rather ridiculously attractive backside.

Unk chuckled and I blushed again, darn it. I really had to get that under control. While the old man winked at me.

"Ah, young love," he said. Before his face fell, sorrow swallowing joy, memory surfacing in a rush, the bubble of it almost taking me.

I had to shake off the connection to keep from diving into the entirety of his life, the lure of living another's memories—especially once I'd done so—a bit like an addiction. Instead, I shifted my focus which meant, instead of his past, I got to see glimpses of his future.

A sad and tragic day unfolded for him in my

mind's eye, flashing forward in an instant while the world stood still around me. Being chased off by a store owner while he scrounged for a bit of food, having his belongings scattered when a car struck his cart, a binge on alcohol that led him to a deep stupor inside a cardboard box as night fell.

Step back, Phoebe. See the bigger picture.

There, branching from this moment, another option. And a second, a third. Infinite possibilities chasing lines of choice and luck spreading in a fan of futures that flickered in hope of creation, waiting for his next decision. Except, it was clear from the solidity of the one I'd just seen he was on a path to choose the worst of his fates, not the best. Not even the next most hopeful.

One thing I knew for sure. His beliefs, his patterns of being, held him in thrall. But I could also see that all it would take to shift him into something more positive was a little nudge.

And so, despite knowing what it would cost me, I tapped into my most powerful—and most frustratingly tempting—power and used the benevolence of synchromysticism to shift his luck.

Just a little, knowing the slightest change in the moment made the biggest difference down the road. Watched as the path before him collapsed into that same flickering possibility as the others, heard the sigh of choice, and exhaled with a whisper of my own.

Instead of dumpster diving behind the restaurant, his path took him to a different place now, a café a block over, a simple decision, the smallest of choices. That owner gave him a sandwich and drink, paused for a kind word which timed his interaction with the person who almost hit his cart instead handing him a ten-dollar bill. And while he still fell into sleep with a bottle in his hand, it was to happy memories and peace.

I'd take it.

And the punishment to follow.

Time started again. Unk blinked at me, his aura now warm and a little pink at the top, the heavy gray softened. He'd never know what I'd done, and I was okay with that.

"Thank you, Miss Monday," he said.

I smiled as he shuffled off, sighing to myself before standing, sketch in hand.

Time to share what I'd learned with the detectives before something terrible happened.

CHAPTER TWO

I made it two steps before I tripped over my shoelace and almost faceplanted into the side of a desk. My sketchbook wasn't so lucky, flying forward and skidding to a stop at the feet of the startled detective who looked up as I caught my balance and shrugged with a weak smile at my clumsiness.

Not my fault, but whatever.

I hurried forward, not seeing the passing officer who, naturally, ran right into me, the fresh cup of coffee he held spilling over the two of us in a shocking hit of heat. We quickly batted at each other with offered napkins from laughing police personnel, my penchant for being a klutz well documented in the department.

I hoped Unk Jay-Jay appreciated his good luck. Because I was in for a very uncomfortable twenty-four hours at his expense. Not that I regretted the choice, not in the least. If the price I paid to ensure the dear old fellow had a chance at some hope was making an idiot of myself, well. I'd pay it and that was that.

The last ten feet I had to cross felt like a minefield, but I made it without further incident, though I was sure the wincing expression on my face was the reason they grinned at me.

Detective Anna Morales handed me my sketchbook, the image I'd drawn already removed for her file. The gorgeous Latino detective who really could have had a successful career as a model sat on the edge of her partner's desk, statuesque height, flawless skin and amber eyes making her a standout. And yet, she usually wore her thick, black hair in a tight ponytail or bun in a no-nonsense way that mirrored her choice of jeans and dress jacket with a fitted button up beneath. Detective Morales broadcasted all business, while the softness of her aura made me adore her for the kind heart within.

"Great job, as usual," Anna said, mild alto cultured and without accent despite the fact I knew she spoke perfect Spanish.

"I'm sorry I couldn't do more." I retrieved the book, instantly dropped it. Sighed just a little, bent to retrieve it again.

At the exact moment she did.

Not quite the sound of cartoon coconuts meeting when we bonked heads, but close enough.

Her partner, Detective Nathan Sallow, guffawed. I'd never heard anyone laugh the way he did, always wondered what an actual guffaw sounded like. Sallow had the market on that term cornered.

"Smooth," he said with a huge grin, leaning back in his creaking office chair, sausage hands folded over the bump of his potbelly, ugly Christmas tree tie so garish it was almost cute loosened at the neck of his unbuttoned collar. Where Morales was a stunning beauty, Sallow had that TVesque slovenly stereotype about him that made me think of old police dramas. "Once more from the top, with feeling this time."

Morales kicked his chair with the toe of her boot, sour expression at his attempt at comedy turning to another smile for me while I carefully stepped back a half pace to distance myself.

I'd managed to pick up the book, at least, so go me. Tucked it into my satchel without incident, yay to that. Was zipping up my puffy coat over my clothes without catching anything important in the closing metal teeth, so hey, wins all around, when Anna spoke.

"Thanks for your hard work," Anna said. "Have a great Christmas."

I perked, remembering what I'd brought, fished in my bag and retrieved the packages my mother prepared. Handed the red one to Anna (without dropping it, Mom's magic at work) and the green one to Sallow. "Merry Christmas."

Sallow tore his open instantly, the first chunk of cinnamon chocolate toffee gone before Anna could say thank you. He groaned his pleasure, savoring it a moment while I relaxed despite my lingering bad luck. Mom's suggestion had been a great one and I was happy she'd tucked the two small boxes into my bag before I'd left the house.

Nice to know she not only approved of my work but liked the normal people I worked with.

I left them then without further mishap, taking my time weaving through the busy space, reaching the foyer of the station in one piece and only slipping once on the steps, toe catching a single tiny patch of ice. Caught myself in time with a mouse squeak and giggle of resignation, only to feel someone's hands catch me when I slid yet again.

Looked up into those amazing green eyes and felt myself heat up inside my winter coat despite the chill in the air.

"You okay?" Coop released me, looking even bigger in his own puffy uniform jacket, blond hair covered in an adorable dark blue toque with the department logo on the front.

I shrugged, tried to laugh it off while my hormones—traitors all—did a shiver dance. Now that I was outside the spell, back in the real world for solid, awkward and well-worn me smothered the genuine version in a layer of embedded familiarity I wished I could shake. "Wouldn't be Phoebe Monday if I didn't make a fool of myself."

Coop's quick frown of denial warmed me further, the sweetie. He could have been pushy about his attraction to me, never was. And that aura. If he glowed with more blues and pinks and lovely yellows, he'd be a saint, I was sure of it.

And he liked me.

Poor boy had no idea.

I really needed to get home and hide in my room for the next day and suffer my punishment where no one would see me collapse in a heap of why me.

"It's pretty cold," he said then. "Do you need a ride?"

I didn't, had walked on my own two feet the ten blocks just an hour ago when it hadn't been this cold and I wasn't cursed with bad luck. Which would now likely mean a very uncomfortable return trip. That I'd earned, don't forget.

"I'm happy to give you a drive." So much hope in those lovely green eyes I didn't hesitate. Who was I kidding? There were a lot of reasons—like his broad shoulders and handsome face and big hands and how he smelled so good—I made the choice I did.

"Sure," I said. "Thank you." Touched his arm on impulse, knew I was smiling like an idiot.

Which was okay. Because so was Coop.

CHAPTER THREE

Coop grinned next to me, the warmth of the police cruiser's interior almost immediate, the squawk of his radio transmitting the occasional call out he ignored—hopefully not to his detriment, though he didn't once seem like he'd chosen me over his job. By the time we reached the brownstone, I had put from my mind the lingering dread that hung over me when I used synchromysticism and triggered my luck's turns for the worse.

Nice not to have to say a word the whole five minute drive, to let Coop chatter on, vague flashes of his plans for Christmas with his parents in the suburbs to his favorite team winning the hockey game, mention of how fun the precinct holiday party had been and he missed seeing me there a welcome layer of normal.

Not that Coop cared I was quiet. I think he liked having someone to talk to. His aura always warmed when I just listened, so I was happy to continue, partly because a lot of my life I wasn't able to divulge anyway. And besides, I loved the sound of his voice.

Liked! *Liked* the sound of his voice. A*hem*.

He parked, engine running, grinning at me. "If I don't see you, Phoebe, have a great Christmas."

"Thanks, Coop." Darn it, why hadn't I asked for three boxes from Mom? He would have loved her candy. Well, maybe it would be an excuse to see him once my bad luck wore off.

"You guys celebrate, right?" He seemed hesitant then, smile failing a little. Sweet of him to think of such things. Not like I could hide the fact we leaned toward an alternative (to us traditional) belief system. "Sorry, I shouldn't assume or anything."

I laughed at that. "As my grandmother says, we're pagans, dear, not savages. Of *course* we celebrate Christmas."

Coop's chuckle made my heart skip. This was a terrible idea and I really should have just gotten out of the car then and there and asked Mom or Isolde or my sister to whip up some kind of spell to help me dodge the bullet—no pun intended—that was Cooper Hudson. After all, my family wasn't known for their prolonged relationship status and the men in the lives of the Monday women tended to either tragic ends, devious betrayals or hideous punishments to last a lifetime.

Mind you, I wasn't a typical Monday, but still. I'd have hated for something to happen to someone as lovely as him.

Instead of the good and kind thing, I stayed put, enjoying him a few moments longer, while he cleared his throat, sudden nerves showing in the sparkling glow of him. A blush crawled through his aura, so apparent my breath caught and I had to smother my a blush myself.

Yes, it was very clear to me he was interested. And yes, it was very clear to me I was conflicted. And yes, not doing something about the situation made me a very bad person. But I'd never had anyone treat me the way Coop did, and he was honestly the nicest guy I'd ever met. So I guess I couldn't blame myself for wanting just a bit more of him in my life despite knowing that was all I'd have.

Coop inhaled abruptly, green eyes wider than normal. "I was wondering..."

Meep.

"My parents have this Boxing Day party," he rushed into the rest like he knew what to expect but couldn't help himself. "I told them about you and they really want to meet you. So, I was wondering if you'd like to come." I'd never heard anyone swallow before. Even without his aura visible, it was clear he'd put himself out there in a way that meant I could either make his day or break his heart.

Thing was, the guy might have been delicious to look at and could have been an arrogant jerk who treated women like objects. I'd certainly met enough men his age—and younger, and older—with that attitude, who let their genetic lottery win carry them instead of working hard, being respectful, open and caring, trusting their own compassion. Part of me knew I needed to say no, though in truth I was the only one who thought so. My family encouraged me, not the other way around. Still, how could I invite the disaster that was a relationship with a normal person when I was so far from ordinary it hurt sometimes?

I caught myself nodding, smiling despite myself. "Thanks," I said. "I'd like that."

I might as well have told him I'd marry him.

"Awesome." He beamed like a small sun, almost puppy wriggling in his seat. "They'll be super excited. I told them what an amazing artist you are."

My turn to squirm. "Thanks for the ride," I said. "Just message me the address and time."

He shook his head with the most adorable of nose wrinkles. "I'll come get you," he said. "It's the least I can do."

This boy. Honestly.

And then he had to go and lean across my lap to the glove compartment of the car and open it, freeing a small box wrapped in beautiful silver foil with a dark blue ribbon and bow hugging the shining paper. When he offered it to me, shy smile already endearing, I took it without thinking, blinking unexpected tears.

"But I didn't get you anything," I said.

Coops face turned serious, and with complete authenticity, he said, "But you give me something every time I see you."

We both laughed at the same moment, in the

same breath, our cheeks matching pink while I kicked my twenty-four-year-old self so she'd stop behaving like a teenager and tucked the box between my mittened hands, against my chest. Honestly, you'd think I lived in a tower and never dated or something. He just… gave me that giddy feeling inside that melted me into a puddle.

"Thank you," I said.

"Merry Christmas, Phoebe," he said.

With nothing left to say, I climbed out, stumbling, naturally, laughing over it though rather than feeling that resigned acceptance I usually did. Coop waved, beeped the horn as I bypassed the front entry to the brownstone's family storefront, The Heathenry and the requisite Christmas décor—a little extravagant thanks to the efforts of my mother.

I turned down the side alley to the sound of Coop driving off.

Maybe I was wrong and the Monday tendency to male inclusion didn't apply to me. Was there a chance I might find a sort of happily ever after with someone like Coop? A nice thing to ponder, and though I'd pretty much exclusively dated guys from my walk of life, the idea of spending the rest of my days with the handsome officer?

More appealing that maybe it should have been.

I almost missed the figure at the end of the alley who leaned into the brick wall, one knee cocked with the sole of his foot pressed behind him, smoking a cigarette past the hoody over his face. The only reason I noticed? Bad luck almost tumbled me to the ground near the door. The near fall meant I half-turned toward the alley and looked up at the right moment.

Had a flash of a memory, and without any control, was suddenly remembering standing in front of him, Unk beside me, in a darker space than this one, reliving what I'd only just left behind with a whoosh of understanding.

Before I could break free, the mysterious young man caught me staring and, tossing his smoke to the ground, strode off in a sudden and hurried stride, out of sight and my reach before I could inhale and reclaim myself.

I had zero proof it was the same young man. And with my luck, I could easily misread what just happened. Probably had. It was simply the proximity of the memory, the state of my power, the familiar look of his dress that drove me back into the recollection I'd shared.

And yet

I unlocked the side door with my mind whirling, wondering if I should call the detectives. Sighed as I realized I really wanted to call Coop. And made the choice to let it go.

After all, I wasn't a police officer. What business did I have chasing a possible suspect? None, that's what. Especially in my condition. I'd only make things worse and maybe damage my relationship with the department. That I couldn't live with. Time to retreat and endure my personal bad luck spell without hurting anyone else.

CHAPTER FOUR

The instant I was in the door, a red, furry beast leapt from the bundle of boots and coats tucked into the nook and snatched the small, shining box I still gripped in my free hand.

I didn't even have time for a squeak and he was gone, poof of a tail flashing as he bounded to the corner and disappeared.

"Jinks!" Like it would do me any good to yell at him. Since when had my house fox ever listened to me? "Get back here with that!" Some days I needed to be reminded why I'd rescued his furry behind when I'd found him abandoned, starving and weak and in need of immediate help. Except as soon as I did remember how I'd come upon the now fit, healthy and utterly playful—and bratty, stubborn and curious—cub, I answered my own question.

Besides, I only had my bad luck to blame. On a good day, I'd have thought to tuck the shiny thing out of sight, knowing Jinks had a fascination with anything sparkly. And anything to do with making me chase him.

If I ever wanted to know what was in the box, I was going to have to recruit help. Which meant telling one or more of the Monday women in my life what happened, where it came from and what I'd agreed to.

Groaned as I realized what I'd agreed to. Was I really going to go to Cooper Hudson's very normal parent's house in the suburbs of Crescent, Washington? Stand around and drink eggnog and eat canapés like I was just folks, be my normal freakish, awkward self and ensure they never, ever invited me back again ever?

That might take care of his attraction to me.

Pondering my terrible error in judgment, I kicked off my boots, hung up my coat—it only took three tries, so there was that—and headed down the hallway in my sock feet, following the path my pet had taken on the off chance he'd grown tired of the game and dropped the box. I wasn't holding my breath, my luck running exactly as expected.

I turned the corner and slipped through the door to the back room of the shop. No sign of Jinks in the storeroom, and neither in the front when I peeked out. Mom had closed early, the front door shuttered, no one behind the counter. While normal people only saw the herbalist and spiritualist dispensary we cultivated for their benefit, my grandmother, Isolde (don't you *dare* call me *Granny*), and Mom had made

The Heathenry the one stop for all things spell craft on the entire West coast.

I retreated, no Jinks to be found, and was almost to the main hall that led to the house when I stumbled over the trim at the threshold and flew headlong toward the far wall. I know I would have struck it if there hadn't been a tall, black-cloaked personage in the way to stop my forward momentum, though I wasn't sure the stately druid liked being my savior.

On the other hand, Silas Gael's soft smile and gentle hands that caught me and held me upright showed nothing of irritation. He'd been around since I could remember, was familiar with my particular idiosyncrasies and had, in fact, attempted to help in the past. I guess I was more judgmental of my failings than anyone else. Go figure that one out and let me know where it gets you.

"Dear Phoebe," Silas said, black eyes sparkling, deeply lined face smiling, tall, lean body looming. Like whatever made him had stretched him out just a bit too thin, though his expression was kindly enough, and he always did his best to make me feel comfortable.

"Sorry, Silas," I said, righting myself. He let me go after a slightly uncomfortable hand-holding moment, bowing from his great height with one of those long-fingered hands pressed to his chest. He'd pushed back his cowl, short, iron gray hair thick and shining in the light in the hall, bushy eyebrows wiggling like active caterpillars over his deep-set black eyes.

"You've been practicing your power," he said, approval in his deep voice, nodding ponderously though I didn't respond past a little wince of guilt.

"My bad," I said.

"To the contrary, dear Phoebe," Silas objected with one slender and overly long index finger raised, the silver ring there flashing with a ruby so dark it was almost black. "One must use the abilities they possess in order to master the consequences as well as the benefits."

"Have you seen Jinks?" Yes, I changed the subject, but I really didn't feel like a deep and heartfelt discussion about my power right now. I wanted to catch the little thief who took my present and find out what was in that box.

"I have not," the old druid said. "I do, however, have something for you." His other hand dipped beneath his cloak and emerged with a small, round runestone, one side etched with a crescent moon, the other, when he flipped it over in his palm, marked with something I didn't recognize. The flat, black stone looked hand carved and polished. "If you would indulge an old spell caster, my dear, perhaps this might be of some assistance in the more personally troubling aspects of your delightful ability?"

I took the stone, felt a tingle in my palm on contact and then nothing. The roof didn't fall in and a hole didn't open in the floor and the world continued spinning, so there was that.

"Thank you," I said, tucking it into my front pocket, pretty sure it wouldn't help, just like every other attempt he'd made to assist, but unwilling to hurt his feelings.

Again with the bow, the faint scent of earth, pine and old forests rising from the folds of his leather and velvet cloak. "A pleasure, as always." One of those eyebrows lifted. "You will keep me apprised?"

I nodded instantly. "Are you here to see Isolde?"

"I have had a word with your mother," he said, "about tonight's Yule celebration." Oh no. I groaned faintly, had forgotten all about the party. Instantly rejected the idea of attending even as Silas tilted his head as he spoke again. "I will, of course, see you there?"

I wasn't going to lie to his face, instead changed the subject again. "I should go find Jinks," I said. "He stole something and if I let him get away with it—"

"Of course," Silas waved me off. "Best of luck to you my dear. And do tell me how things work out."

Rather than answer, knowing it was a bit rude, I spun and hurried off, heading down the long hall separating the main house from the shop, taking the last door and entering the kitchen with some trepidation.

I had to tell Mom I wasn't going to Yule. Not going to end well. Big breath drawn against the inevitable disappointment she'd use against me, I pushed through the door to the sound of my mother singing.

CHAPTER FIVE

And stopped, exhaled, inhaled all the amazing, divine, deliriously decadent smells that surrounded me while my happy mother stood in the middle of the kitchen and sang her power into the food she created.

I stood for a long moment, grinning and hugging myself, enjoying the view. Mom was beautiful, had always been beautiful, with her full, black curls, her deep blue eyes, flawless skin and sultry voice. Time and two babies had filled out her hips and chest giving her the most voluptuous silhouette, all witch under her midnight blue velvet skirt and flowing white blouse, those curls caught back from her damp face with a bright blue band, cheeks glowing, her entire being glowing, while pots and jars and decanters and spices bobbed around her in a dance of ingredients that responded to the compelling music of her voice.

Three pans filled with some kind of batter were already prepped for the oven, it looked like, four trays of candies set aside on the butcher block, tins piled up on the side board out of the way, ready for tonight. Mom might have been a fantastic cook, but her baking? Utterly legendary.

I hadn't meant to interfere, I swear it. I had no intention of getting in her way. I'd spent hours as a little girl, even as a teenager, and occasionally now as an adult, sitting on a stool in this very kitchen, ultra modern white and stainless steel since the massive renovation Mom delighted in, watching her work. Joining in on her song from time to time, usually with her encouragement, though I never could quite match her and my creations were only okay, not the addictive and mouth-wateringly satisfying treats she came up with.

And never, ever did I do so when on a streak of bad luck. I knew better. And yet, this moment, walking into the unexpected, after memory had played a big part of my day already, I found myself sinking into the past's arms as easily as I could have hers, and without thinking about it, I opened my mouth and sang.

I will not describe the chaos I created, because I am too ashamed of the disaster that erupted from my clumsy interference. Know only that, less than a minute later, I sat on the floor of the hall outside the kitchen door, panting and sweating, Mom collapsing next to me, smoke billowing out from under the threshold, the sound of pots and pans thudding against the portal making the house shake while something truly unhappy roared its lack of enthusiasm at being summoned in the middle of Mom's souffle.

Tears threatened, my throat tight, regret and guilt overwhelming me. I could barely look at her, mumbled an apology while shaking, not from fear, but utter disillusionment. Why had I not just done as I'd said and gone to my room?

Mom, for her part, blew the stray curl that escaped her headband out of her astonished and gleaming eyes and laughed, hugging me in her warm embrace, strong and soft and smelling of all things yummy while rocking me a little, seeming unconcerned by the raging demon demanding in a booming voice something I couldn't understand because it wasn't English. She paused a moment, flickered her fingers with a faint frown and a whispered, "Oh, hush," and the voice reduced in volume and pitch until it was just an uninspiring series of demands in a mouse's hilarious squeak. "There," she said, beaming at me. "Oh, sweet girl, you used your power today!" She hugged me again, rocking me a little. "I'm so proud of you for helping people even though you know what it will cost you." Morgade Monday might have been an all-powerful and formidable witch to the rest of our world, the Mother to my sister's Maiden and my grandmother's Crone, but she would always just be my mom to me.

"I'm so sorry," I said, choking on the familiar apology.

"Hush, my dearest darling," Mom said, stroking my short, dark hair with one hand, cheek resting on the top of my head, singing softly under her breath while her power sifted over me, gentle and kind, and my need to cry faded even if my guilt did not.

To be honest, there were times when Mom treating me like I was still ten made me wonder if it was time to move out. This wasn't one. I could have sat there in her arms and let her comfort me for a lot longer than I did. Except, of course, I wasn't a little girl, I was a woman and she had work to do.

Work I'd more than interrupted.

I pulled away, kissed her cheek. "I'd offer to help," I said.

Mom laughed, falling back into the wall, looking almost drunk with the power she'd been using, flush with all that energy. "It's nothing I can't handle," she said, taking my hand, stroking the back with her other fingertips. "Besides, that was fun."

Of course she'd think so. "Have you seen Jinks?" Yes, I was still thinking about the box.

A quick frown that didn't touch her smile and an inquisitive eye arch and I had to confess what happened. The only way she could really help was if I gave her all the information. Holding back on a detail—like who the box was from—would interfere with the magic. Which made keeping secrets from my family? Pretty much impossible.

"What a sweet boy," Mom said, a bit too suggestively which had me blushing and pulling my hand away while she laughed deep and sultry. She did sit up, though, and focused, staring into space while she summoned that singular power of hers, the source of the abiding dominion of the Monday women.

Some called it being psychic, normals who could, if clumsily and never for long, tap into the source of all. To us, it was wonderworking, clear visions of the past, present and future unwinding out before the three women I adored so much. My version might have offered possibilities but theirs saw truths. The fact I could tap into all three with my talent—bits and pieces of the Monday inherited power showing up in my visions of the past as memory, my influence over the present in the luck I could bestow and the unfolding of the future through the pathways of possibility I could see—always excited my mother, though I could never find a reason for it, nor a real purpose. Sure, I might be able to help others in small nudges, but when I had to weigh it against the price? Sometimes didn't seem worth it. And certainly nothing compared to the awesomeness the three women in my life had control over. After all, when Mom saw the present—her particular ability while she was the Mother—there was no vacillating on what could be. Just the world as it was.

Mom finally returned to me, the minor magic tied to the massiveness of the Mother lingering in her, shaking her head with a tiny sigh more accepting than judging. "I'm sorry, sweet girl," she said. "Perhaps it's the lingering effects of your casting, but I can't find the item you seek. And you do know

Jinks has his own odd ways about him." All animals did, though Jinks seemed even less susceptible to magical control than typical creatures. Contrary brat. She patted my hand and I stood, knowing the moment was over, helping her to her feet where she brushed at the mess of her skirt before snapping her fingers with a, "Get thee gone, stain," and was suddenly clean again.

I hugged her, kissed her cheek. Hesitated then chose to stay quiet. I'd tell her about Yule later. I'd already done enough, right?

Mom let me go, reaching for the doorknob. I turned, the room blocked by the open door, to see her, determined and commanding, gesture into the kitchen with one hand. "Down, foul batter!" With that, she stormed the castle, the door slamming behind her.

I left her to her battle, knowing she'd come out triumphant, keeping my head down and my hands to myself as I hurried to the entry again and up the stairs to the main house, winding one story further to the sleeping level, my bedroom door calling me to come and be safe behind it's shielding presence.

I almost made it. Was *this* close. Only to be tackled from behind as I opened the way to my room, thrown headlong forward in an aggressive attack I should have seen coming.

CHAPTER SIX

I had enough momentum I made it to the bed, falling onto it with the full weight of my assailant on my back. Her giggling kind of ruined the moment, truth be told, and though I was the younger, Selene rarely showed it. Twenty-six or not, she had the heart of a teenager and while on a good day I would be ready for whatever she had to dish out in her devilish and prankster heart, today was not that day.

No complaining on my part, either. I really needed my sister right now. When she finally rolled off me and tucked her hand under her cheek, laying next to me and smiling that gorgeous smile of hers, I impulsively hugged her before letting her go again, the tears Mom successfully drove away surfacing one more time.

"Tell me," Selene whispered, brilliant blue eyes huge, thick, blonde hair pooling around her in a cascade of spun gold, porcelain cheeks pink with excitement, "about your day."

I did. I told her everything, from my visit in the morning to the studio where I kept most of my artwork these days, hanging out with my best friend, Pickle, how he'd been experimenting with a new shade of green for his hair to match the Christmas onesie he now favored over everything else in life, my journey to the police station and the encounter with Unk Jay-Jay. I tried skimming over Coop, but Selene knew my ways and poked me when I mentioned him in passing, all fake casual.

"Spill," she said. "Everything about the pretty boy."

She was such a *girl*. Which made me giggle and gush over how handsome he was and the way he smelled and oh my mother moon how his rear end couldn't possibly look that good in his uniform pants and be real. Selene's wicked grin came as my reward while she wriggled on the bed and urged me on. She really was the worst influence. Not that I was complaining or anything.

I received the requisite oohs and ahhs from my description of the sketch experience, the memory Unk shared with me, the drawing's unsatisfying completion. She lingered over my drive home with Coop, however, and when I told her about his response to my not getting him a present?

Well. I might as well have sent her to the moon for real.

Selene squealed and rolled over onto her back, hands clasped over her heart, turning her head to look at me with that ridiculous longing look of hers that would have every male in the room—if there were any—begging her to let them do something for her just to see her smile. "How ro*man*tic," she said. "He's so good for you." Again with the wickedness. "Why haven't you kissed him yet."

I snorted and smacked her hip while she laughed at me.

"Stop that," I said. "You know why." Sighed despite myself, though I never meant to. "We just don't do that sort of thing."

"We don't." Selene nodded, serious suddenly, a rarity for my sister. "Me, Mom, Isolde. But you can, sugarplum. I'm sure of it."

I exhaled a little, hating to ask. "You've seen it?" The future was, after all, her wonderwork.

Selene winked but didn't answer. She never did. Instead, looked me up and down with curiosity and eagerness. "So, where is it?"

I groaned when I realized what she was looking for and finished my story with such hangdog determination—just to make her laugh—she was gasping and grinning and giggling all over again.

When I finished with the mess I made in the kitchen, Selene hooted. "You summoned a demon in Mom's souffle?" She smacked the quilt with both open palms, kicking her feet while I covered my mouth with both hands to keep from snorting again. Something about my eternally sunny sister always made me feel like a kid, too, but less in the way Mom's attention did. That I fought a bit, protested internally. Selene's silliness? Freed me to just have fun for a bit.

She finally sobered, rolling over again, meeting my eyes with her shining ones, button nose wrinkling. "I love you, BeeBee," she whispered.

Now I was going to cry. Not that she didn't tell me all the time how much she loved me, because she did. I guess I was just on the verge and tears seemed logical. So I let them fall but smiled anyway.

"Love you too, Selene."

She reached over, took my hand. "Let's see if we can find the box." Looked away, stared at the ceiling with her stunning face in repose. While I fought off a moment of weakness that surprised me but probably shouldn't have. Not like I hadn't had these feelings before. Because naturally there were times I compared myself—short, slim, dark hair, gray eyes, rather unremarkable despite being pretty enough—to my tall, slender, graceful and utterly glorious sister. She would have hated knowing it, protested instantly I was the most beautiful woman in the whole world and the best sissy and don't be a ridiculous ninny, BeeBee. That was part of the problem. Selene was the Maiden, at least for now, the perfect woman who not only held her own perfection in utter authenticity but radiated it and passed it on to every woman in her sphere.

Hard not to want to be her sometimes. Especially when I was the extra child in the family, the singular female offspring beside me almost two years old when my very surprised mother conceived me.

Unheard of in our lineage, a second daughter. And though they never, ever made me feel like I was unwanted, unloved, it remained that I was outside who they were—Crone, Mother, Maiden, wonderworkers of the Moon—and always would.

Selene sighed, released the power, turned to me again. Took note, I think, of how my mood had shifted, but didn't make a big deal of it. Instead, she blinked slowly, as though still in the Maiden, before speaking. "You will find the gift," she said, voice a little echoey and modulated, the voice of her power, "but only at the chosen time." She shook her head, shrugged. "Whatever that means."

I had to laugh at her casual discarding of the massive power she wielded. "Thanks."

Now it was her turn for her own excitement as she sprang from the bed, twirling so her full, cream skirt belled around her, tiny pink twinset hugging her slim curves, those glossy golden waves of hers reminding me of a fairy-tale princess, always. She didn't need a tiara to look the part. "You have to help me pick," she gushed. "I have it down to three dresses, but I can't decide." Selene eye rolled at herself, cocking one hip, hand on it, waggling her index finger at me. "No judging your poor, elderly sister. I know I'm being a girl. I'm allowed."

Right. Yule. "I'm happy to help," I said, sitting up crossed legged on my bed while she squealed and ran from the room, appearing a moment later with an armload of what looked like way more than three dresses.

The next hour was a parade of one after another of truly lovely outfits she donned behind my changing screen, while I ix-nayed or approved of her choices. Mostly it was random because she looked fantastic in everything, though it seemed I read her body language right because she finally had it down to two—the third from her original trio long gone— the fitted blue dress with the slit up the side at war with the pale cream wrap of the softest angora, trimmed in pearls.

"You know you're going to pick the fluff," I said.

Selene winked, stroking the soft fur-like fabric. "Fine," she said. "If you say so." Collapsed next to me one more time. "Now, what are you wearing?"

Ah, yes. The talk. "I'm not going tonight," I said as softly and yet clearly and with sincere determination as I could manage.

She didn't waver in her stare, still smiling. "So, maybe the new red dress?" Selene stood, went to my closet, opened it, starting pulling out things I didn't even know were in there. Caught the deception.

"Looks like I've been the target of the shopping fairy," I said, impossible to keep the sarcasm from my voice.

"This one is *divine*," Selene said, throwing a little black dress at me. I batted it out of my way and scowled at her while she shook out a long-sleeved navy jumpsuit. "What was I thinking?" She tossed it into the closet and retrieved a slinky red number. Which I instantly nixed.

"Selene." She ignored me. "Se*lene*." More

ignoring, more digging, more perusing. "I'm not going."

When she turned back to me, her smile was gone, shoulders a little slumped. Anyone else? I would have accused them of manipulation. My sister, on the other hand, just didn't have it in her. She fought her disappointment like she did everything else. With her whole person. "I heard you," she said.

"My luck is off," I said, having worked out the excuse I needed before talking to Mom and now trying it out on my sister. "You know I'm not the best flyer under normal circumstances." That was an understatement. I'd been known to crash, fall, take others with me in horrific broom collisions. The only solution we'd come up with was to realize any flying I would do could only happen on the creations of others, since every besom I made turned into a deathtrap. Trouble was? "You know your old broom hates me." Hated. Me. With a passion. Obeyed, but to the letter. So if I wasn't super, uber specific? I could—and often did—end up in extremely compromising positions.

Try negotiating with a witch's besom and get back to me. I'll wait.

"And now," I went on, going for hang dog and succeeding at last, "with my bad luck added on? I won't survive the flight."

Selene perked. "You could ride with me." Problem solved in her world.

"I'd hate to see you crash because of me," I said. Really meant it.

My sister looked like she had further arguments and suggestions, but didn't get to deliver them. A floating ball of light passed through my door and came to hover over the end of my bed, bursting like a bubble full of smoke, releasing the words trapped inside.

"Phoebe," my grandmother's spell said in her voice. "Come."

Which meant the silliness with my sister was now over.

Selene kissed me as I rose to follow the summons, hugged me. "You're coming," she whispered, pinched my cheek.

Hard not to sigh as I left, heading for the stairs and the top floor, and the old woman who waited.

I paused at the bottom of the steps when my phone buzzed in my pocket, checked the message from Detective Morales.

Three more homeless attacks, she sent. *Sketches tomorrow?*

I returned an affirmative response, tucking my phone away again, frowning into the quiet of the dark stairwell as I remembered the young man at the end of the alley. Not that I worried about our house or my family. The wards alone around this place would keep any normal out. And the formidable trio I lived with would leave any intruder a smear on the ground before thinking twice. But the fact someone was targeting the homeless? That made me angry. No one had the right to harm the helpless.

My power might not be the awesome magic my

family could summon, but sharing what I had was, as I was taught, the least I could do.

Still thinking about my unusual and yet satisfying job with the police, I headed up the polished wooden stairs to the top floor where my grandmother waited for me.

CHAPTER SEVEN

The wide, black door at the top was closed, as usual, the entire fourth floor Isolde Monday's sole domain. I knocked politely, ignoring the rather rude brass depiction of the male form's more private parts offered up as a knocker. It used to make me giggle as a girl and still managed to make me smile even now, especially when the power she'd infused into the small figure with his oversized nether regions wriggled his hips suggestively when I failed to utilize the obvious, opting for my own knuckles, thanks.

He gave up with a head toss as the door opened of its own accord, the dim entry on the other side making me blink to adjust my vision.

Which, naturally, meant the moment I stepped across the threshold, the toe of my sneaker caught the edge of the thick carpeting and sent me to my hands and knees. At least the heavy pile saved me from permanent damage, but I hit hard enough the heels of both palms ached and I managed somehow to tear a hole in the knee of my jeans.

Well, such rips were trendy, weren't they? Made me wonder, as I shook off the little adrenaline hit that came from the fall, if Unk Jay-Jay was having a good day. I certainly hoped it was worth it.

Eyes now accustomed to the low light, every window shrouded in blackout curtains and only the dim bulbs in the elaborate light fixtures hanging low throughout the open space offering the faintly purple-tinted illumination my grandmother preferred. I slipped out of my sneakers and left them at the door, sock feet sinking into the lush carpeting, walking past the sitting area with its antique velvet upholstered furniture in the deepest plum, not bothering to check the library where shelves climbed to the ceiling, the heavy wooden ladder on its metal wheels an old plaything from my childhood. How many times had I ridden that ladder back and forth across the wall, fetching books at Isolde's teasingly stern command when she could easily have magicked them to her?

I loved this part of the house, but didn't get to visit nearly often enough. Far from a recluse, my grandmother simply preferred her own company—and that of our family, these days. At least, if she was to be believed.

Not surprisingly, I found her at last in the large front space she used for her boudoir, lounging on a daybed, draped in her favorite black silk and fur trimmed gown, silver hair piled on her head in casual elegance, jewelry flashing on every finger as she sampled delicacies from a black box sitting next to her. The memory of jumping on her gigantic bed, the heavy black drapes pulled back, silk-covered pillows flying everywhere, made me smile as I approached, pausing at the edge of her favorite domain.

The small hamster cage, gilded in silver and leaf filigree, rattled where it perched on a stand next to her. "Phoebe!" My grandfather jumped up and down, squeaking my name, the homunculus Isolde had made of the man who fathered my mother rattling the cage in his excitement. "Hello, Phoebe!"

"Hi, Humphrey." There had been a time I'd been fascinated by the tiny, now elderly, gentleman in the cage, his three-piece suit and spectacles and perfectly shaped beard maintained through my grandmother's magic. As I grew older, his circumstance made me sad. Now? He was simply a part of our family in the only way my grandmother would allow. Not to mention the fact I'd discovered he'd tried to kill her and my mother and betray us all. Perhaps the punishment didn't fit the crime, a lifetime spent in a cage, though how was it any different than a normal prison?

My grandmother didn't look up as I waited for her to notice me, regal face elaborately made up, eyes perfectly lined and smoked out, lips her favorite shade of oxblood. When she turned the page on the book she held with a languid gesture, I cleared my throat to catch her attention.

I'd played this game with her since I could

remember, and fought a grin when she looked up as though surprised to find me standing there.

"Ah," she said, waving me toward her. "Phoebe. Come here, child." I joined her on the daybed, sinking down beside her, placing the box of chocolates in my lap and sampling one. She watched me with her vivid blue eyes hooded, before taking one of her own. "Why are you bothering me again?"

"You wanted to see me," I said around a mouthful of Mom's best dark chocolate, batting my eyelashes at her.

She swatted me before tilting her chin upward and resuming her down-the-nose stare at the book in her other hand. "I can't imagine," she said. "I'm far too busy for the likes of you."

I leaned in, scanning the first line of the page she was on and giggled. "Reading erotica again?"

Her head snapped around, lips twitching. "It's educational." She tossed the book at me then, smile widening. "I think you need it more than I do if you're going to continue to moon over that young police officer you can't seem to get enough of."

Today was a day for pink cheeks and splutters. "He's just a friend," I said.

She stared at me a long, silent moment. Then winked.

I leaned in, kissed her cheek. "Love you, Isolde," I said.

She snuggled me closer, warm lips on my temple. "You're having a bad day, darling."

"That's the price," I said into her furry collar.

"We all pay it, one way or another."

Isolde sighed deeply, nodding. "And some of us more than others." Was she talking about herself? Or me? "Ruining your mother's baking won't save you from coming to the Yule celebration, you brat."

I sat up, about to protest, but my grandmother just laughed, a low and lovely sound. Sniffed at me a moment, nose twitching, expression flat.

"Silas," she said. "What did he give you?" Not a question, but a command.

I instantly pulled out the rune stone and handed it to her. My grandmother examined it a moment then huffed, returning it to me with a tsk of disapproval, bangles layered on her wrist tinkling together.

"Druids need to mind their own business," she said, "when it comes to matters of witches." Never mind they'd been friends since childhood and she often conferred with him. "Clearly it's helping." She let one finger glide over the knee of my jeans, knitting the fibers back together as though they had never torn. "Men." She dismissed him with that single word. Then pointed at the large dressing room doors just past her feet. "Go and be useful," she said. "Fetch that which I've made you, oh most unruly of children." Her eyes sparkled when I stood, curious, and did as she asked. Opened the heavy door by the elaborate silver handle and peeked inside.

Selene came by her clothing fetish honestly. The inside of my grandmother's closet was magical, and not just because of the contents. The wonders she'd accumulated over the years all resided within the bigger on the inside warehouse-like space she required to maintain her collection of dresses, shoes, brooms, hats, and who knew what—I'd found a coat of armor once as a child, along with a carriage and three statues of some guy I'd never seen before and later figured were probably not statues—Isolde Monday treasured.

Fortunately, I didn't have far to look for the item in question because a full search would have taken a Sherpa guide, provisions for a week and a compass. Instead, I found myself gasping in surprise at the purple bow-wrapped box that stood at the entry with my name sparkling in lights across the front.

"Bring it here," she said.

I carried the long, slim present, taller than me, though practically weightless, out of the closet and to my grandmother. She swung her legs to the floor, patting the daybed's velvet upholstery for me to sit next to her and guided the box across both our laps.

"I was going to save this for your Christmas present," she said, "but when I felt how your day turned out, it made sense to give it to you a bit early."

The wonderwork of the Crone, seeing the past, had either given her the heads up, or my disaster with Mom downstairs did the trick. I squeezed her hand with a murmured thank you.

"My very dear," she said, voice a little thick, all of the love I knew she had for me showing in her still stunning face, radiating out from her to embrace me though she barely touched me physically, "please know how special you are to us, no matter what others believe of our lineage." Was she reading my mind? She promised she'd stop that. I didn't protest, though, as she went on. "Our hearth wouldn't be the same without you and I have no doubt whatever fate the Great Mother has in store for you and the power you wield, you will do so with grace and in the best interest of your family and those you seek to help."

Crying again? No complaints. "Love you, Isolde."

"Yes, sweet brattiness," she said. "Now open your present, there's a good monster."

I laughed, knew I would miss our game when it was through, refused to think that way right now, and pulled free the shining bow, tipping up the lid and peeking inside.

My grandmother was known for many things, including her no-cares-to-give attitude, her incredible power, her commanding presence. And, in high demand that she rarely and selectively agreed to, as the finest broom maker in existence.

She'd tried to teach me and I'd failed. Knew she was disappointed I wouldn't follow her footsteps, and that Selene's lack of interest meant neither of her granddaughters would take over when she was gone. I'd never, ever, dreamed of asking her to make me a broom when she'd attempted to impart her wisdom, her ability, on me. Had lived with the horrible creations I'd made over the years, finally settling on using the one Selene made as a teenager.

Knowing I'd never be a good flyer, and really only needed it four times a year anyway.

What lay within the box? Took my breath away.

Most witch besoms were practical things, ash or oak and twine or willow and the occasional embellishment with etchings or feathers in the birch bristles. It was the power inside that held the key, the connection between vehicle and witch that mattered. My grandmother, however, refused convention, in case you missed it. Her brooms were works of supernatural art.

She'd magicked it black, shining and polished from the wood of an oak tree, the humming feeling of age from the kind old soul that supplied the beautiful base still linked to its parent growing happy and healthy who knew where. Her power shaped the saddle into a flatter, dipped surface, conformed to the human body, and had a smoothed, saddle-like edge that encouraged side riding if I so chose. Lines of sparkling metal chased in protective patterns and spell work from the silver-capped tip to the thick wire binding the birch bundle to the base. Sapphires winked in curving spirals, as though the tree itself had grown them, the seamless melding of metal, gem and oak drawing the eye to the impressively fanned tail of bristles. Each spun in a curved curl as though twisted individually and melded, in turn, with strings of silver, creating a playfully wistful accent to the far end of the besom.

The best part? The happy and ancient song of its power that called out to me while I sat there and stared at the stunning thing she'd created for me.

"Go ahead," she said. "It's made for you and only you. The only broom you'll ever need."

I turned and hugged her, tears unleashed, heart about to burst. "Thank you," I choked. "Isolde, thank you so much."

She hugged me back, hard enough I had trouble breathing but I didn't care. When she released me, Isolde wiped at the wetness on her own cheeks before slapping my leg.

"Now I have to redo my face before we go," she growled. "And here I did something nice for you."

I scrubbed at my own tears with the sleeve of my sweater, unable to stop smiling. Finally turned back to the besom that sat there, waiting for me to claim it. Hesitated at the last second, my fingers hovering over it. Glanced at my grandmother with a bubble of anxiety smothering my joy.

"What if I ruin it?" More tears, though these had nothing to do with happiness or gratitude. Just that deeply embedded worry there was something wrong with me because I wasn't supposed to be, was I?

My grandmother stared back at me, all masks gone, without guile or humor. "You couldn't possibly," she said. "For you are perfect just as you are, Phoebe, daughter of the Moon. Take your gift, child."

I did, then, fingers stroking the polished wood, feeling the song of the oak turn to a momentary crescendo of joy as it linked into me then settled, burbling a bit its happiness we were finally together.

"I've embedded you in its heart," Isolde said, one long, black-painted nail pointing to a swirl of what had to be a lock of my hair, now wound into and made part of the hand holds at the thinner end. "Double protection spells for the worst of your days when you are forced to endure the opposite of what you gift. Sure flight, level and true. Guidance unerring to every destination. Safe landings in weather and darkness." She showed me each of the runes as she spoke, pointing them out so they glowed at the attention. "In silver, your element, to ensure your binding. Sapphire, your stone, to seal its soul to your bidding." Paused at the final rune near the top of the seat. "And ever home, so you will always find your way back to us." That rune glistened a moment as her power touched it.

"This is amazing," I said. "I don't know how to thank you."

"Come to Yule," my grandmother said, sealing my fate. Her plan in the beginning, more than likely, though I knew it wasn't just convention or personal preference that had her asking. We were a hearth, stronger together despite what I might sometimes think. "Be with your family and celebrate the chance at new beginnings."

I hugged her again, then stood, broom in hand, the box disappearing when she whispered to it.

"Now, off with you, pesky bit of a thing," she said, the game resumed, her attitude returning as she reclined once again with her book and chocolates. "I'm tired of your chatter. Begone."

I left her as she fed my grandfather a sweet, my new besom murmuring happily in my hands, while Isolde chided Humphrey for being such a bad boy.

CHAPTER EIGHT

I huddled inside my black cloak against the chill of the night air, the fur cowl tucked over the updo Selene insisted on creating for me out of a mix of magic and hair pieces she dug out of her collection of costumes and accessories. I missed my cropped bob swinging around my cheeks, the tension and poking of the bobby pins she'd affixed her creation with jabbing me and creating a dull aching where they pulled just a bit too hard.

Not that I'd ever complain, the final result quite lovely and a sweet gesture on my sister's part. Considering the fact I was kind of all thumbs and bumbling—especially now—when it came to anything to do with makeup, hair or fashion meant she got to engage in her game with me—dress up doll time.

Which meant I did end up wearing the silver sheath with the chain halter hooked around my neck to hold up the scooped front while my poor feet suffered inside the strappy chrome sandals she'd squealed over.

Eyeshadow, eye liner, mascara, foundation, powder, bronzer, highlighter, blush, lipstick… by the time she was done with me I hardly recognized myself, more porcelain doll than person.

And then we were bundling into our heavy fur cloaks, my new broom vibrating eagerly in my hand, Mom and Selene taking ample time on the roof of our brownstone to wax poetic over the beauty of its creation—while my grandmother beamed and grumbled to the contrary they were wasting time—before we mounted and rose, the selection of my mother's cooking lashed to a pair of small besoms she'd created for that purpose tethered to her with magic.

I'd never enjoyed flying, not from the moment I'd first sat on a broom. Neither in the company of another or on my own, always afraid of the ultimate splat that awaited at the bottom of the ride. Wherever my fear of heights had come from, no magic my mother mustered or encouragement my grandmother offered, no support and tireless training my sister supplied could free me from my rather unorthodox dislike of anything to do with soaring through the air on the back of a spindly piece of oak that was really, if you thought about it, meant to stay on the ground where it belonged.

After all, if the Great Mother wanted me to fly, she'd have given me wings, as the saying goes.

Tonight? Felt different. I still inhaled and had trouble releasing the breath as the broom responded to my whispered command to rise, the sparkling runes ticking on in little flashes of glittering light while the spells embedded in the shaft came to life. But instead of abject terror and second guessing, I experienced only breathless anxiety when the steadfast and humming besom surrounded me in its rumbling protection and took off like a shot in the midst of my hearth's flight.

So, this was what flying was supposed to feel like.

The novelty kind of wore off about five minutes in, our long trip ahead—though the standing stones site in southern California would have taken far longer without magic—really only an hour but quickly turning into that kind of humdrum hang on and let the broom do its work that left me to think all over again about the splat I'd make.

Except, for the first time, my fear abated and faded and finally left me and I was able to look around, appreciate the night sky, the smile on Selene's face when she skidded through the air next to me, the sound of my mother singing our way to the Yule celebration as warming as the spell embedded in my cloak.

I'd never felt like a true part of our hearth like this before and wondered if maybe, despite my power, my luck actually might have been turning after all.

Hard not to think about Jinks, the missing box, my decision to trust Selene out of my hands at the moment. He'd vanished without a trace and I knew from experience I wouldn't find him again until he was ready.

Still, I really wanted to know what was in the box.

Flying typically felt like forever. This time, the hour quite literally flew by and, before I knew it—and with a faint hint of regret, imagine that—I felt us descend, the shining lights of the Yule fires reaching up toward us, welcoming us to the vast estate on the shores of the Pacific.

We weren't the first to arrive, nor the last, the front drive of Richmond House filled with arriving witches on their own brooms, with servants fetching offerings brought by the party goers, druids and wizards and sorcerers arriving in puffs of air, flashes of light, spots of shadow, everyone chattering amongst themselves while moving at a steady pace toward the massive front steps of the towering stone mansion and the wide-open doors leading into the brightly lit interior.

I held back a bit, staying on Selene's heels as a servant hurried forward in a tux and white gloves, smiling and nodding so his slicked, black hair caught the light from the house, the slits of his eyes narrowing to thin lines in the burning brightness of the Yule fires that roared in giant concrete pots around the perimeter of the driveway.

Hard to hand over my new broom, its matching murmur of regret and promise of another flight actually making me grin. The servant helped me with my cloak and then spun, flashing out with my possessions in hand, leaving me exposed in that silly dress and shoes with my hair making my scalp itch and wondering yet again why I came.

Except, of course, Selene was there, her arm through mine, Mom in her sparkling red velvet gown giving serious and strict instructions to the pair of servants who nodded to her over the still floating besoms supporting her creations, while my grandmother stared at the house like it offended her, tall, slender body still shapely despite her age, sheathed in a floor-length slip of jet silk with the biggest, fullest feather I'd ever seen standing up from her pile of silver curls.

Selene was, of course, stunning in cream and pearls as I knew she'd be, tugging me along toward the house, following Mom and Isolde inside, pulling me to a stop with a small giggle when the official at the door drew a breath through his jutting tusked underbite, squiggle tail wriggling outside his black dress pants, hooved feet gleaming.

"Your attention!" His voice echoed, augmented with magic, bright, black eyes settling on me a moment. "Make welcome their most honorable and exalted, the Triunity of the Great Moon, bearers of the wonderworks, the magnificent witches Monday!"

I'd never get used to being introduced like that because he wasn't talking about me, was he? A smattering of applause followed his announcement, signaling our freedom to no longer be the center of attention and enter the foyer at last. This was one of the reasons I really didn't like Yule. If it had been a simple matter of a ceremony, Mom's food, some wine, a little dancing around a fire? I'd be all for it. Except, of course, that wasn't how things went for witches like us.

Oh, how I loved being stared at, whispered about as we walked by, knowing everything about us was under scrutiny because this was hardly my first Yule celebration, or any other that required us to endure society. Selene was my only saving grace, to be honest, her cheery and sunny disposition either a mask she chose to hide behind when faced with the truly epic envy I felt pummel me from all sides, only matched by the vibrating hunger of those who wanted a piece of us—my family, that was—and the simpering ass kissing that barely hid the desperate needs that would be laid at the feet of the wonderworkers before the night was over.

At least I was spared any of it directly. The first few years I'd been old enough to understand the goals of the varied types of attention aimed at us, my discomfort often led me to hide behind Mom's skirts or go find a closet to sit in until everything was over. Not that I'd resorted to that for a long time. Still, I had fond feelings for closets, those dark and quiet places where one could be themselves with no one looking.

Which naturally made me even more of a weirdo than I'd already been.

Selene clutched at my arm with a gasp when she led me past the main foyer and a knot of young witches drinking champagne and pretending not to give us the up and down with their nasty side-eye, past the arch toward the main ballroom. "He's here," she whispered, cheeks flushed, pupils dilating before letting me go, spinning on me with the kind of intensity that had me smirking. "How do I look?"

"Oh, please," I said, "you know you're the most beautiful woman here and Jericho Richmond doesn't stand a chance against you." I peeked in the direction she refused to look, spotting him not too far away, looking stunningly gorgeous in his white tux jacket and tie, jet hair tousled in that casually careful way of his, violet eyes rising to meet mine. I threw him a cheeky grin and a wave while Selene hissed at me.

"Oh you did not, you brat," she breathed. "Is he coming over?" So hilarious how she refused to look, posed and poised, the Maiden shining through her eyes. She'd been cultivating this capture for almost a year now, had pegged him—with the blessing of his family and ours—for her transition from her present power to Mom's, as was the way of things.

"You'd think you were in a hurry to be the Mother," I said, winking. "Feeling matronly, are we, sissy?"

She swatted at me, laughed. "Silly," she said, "I have lots of time for that to happen. But no one said I couldn't have some fun before I have to move on." Her laugh escaped in a throaty warble that, naturally, was the sound Jericho walked into when he came to a halt next to us.

If he'd been smitten with Selene before? That seductive chuckle sealed the deal.

I might as well have been a piece of furniture as he reached out, took her hand, lifted it to his lips. Not a word spoken between them. Only my sister staring into his eyes and vice versa and a sort of heated wave of oh dear washing over the two of them and out into the general vicinity that sent me scrambling backward and out of their mutual reach so I didn't blush myself to death.

Giving my bad luck the opportunity to hook the heel of one sandal on the toe of another party-goer's shoe and send me toppling backward in slow motion, my mouth an O of well crap and my arms wind milling to no avail.

Only to be caught in mid fall by a pair of strong arms. The scent of cinnamon and coffee and maple and something spicy hit me the moment his touch did as my rescuer, in a flourish of heroics, turned my near disaster into a dip that swept my breath from my lungs the moment those intense ice blue eyes met mine.

CHAPTER NINE

"I'd love to dance," he said before sweeping me back into a upright position, his head of height over mine putting him in a perfect position to look down into my eyes, his lips just over my open mouth.

Why did this total stranger feel so familiar?

"Ah, Phoebe." Silas's interruption was almost annoying, though considering my luck, any attraction I felt to tall, dark and dreamy was likely going to end badly. "So lovely to see you again." Silas hadn't changed out of his druidic attire, though he'd donned a heavy silver necklace over his plain, black shirt and pants, his cloak gone wherever mine had been taken. "I see you've finally met my nephew."

"Not entirely, uncle," my rescuer said. "Elias Gael, at your service."

Ah, that must have been the connection I was feeling, that oddly eerie familiarity I had to fight to ignore. I stuck out one hand to the handsome young man who looked down at it with a half smile before taking it in his own strong one. "Phoebe Monday," I said, trying to shake only to have my palm turned upward, brought to his lips, brushed every so gently while those crisp blues devoured me all over again.

It should have been flattering, to be treated the way my sister had been when I rarely had that kind of attention aimed in my direction from an equally attractive magic user with potential I knew my family would approve of. It did cross my mind it was odd, perhaps, I'd never met him before, since I'd known Silas my entire life. But I was more distracted by the sudden feeling—a bright, sharp shift from, *hello handsome* to *things that made me hmmm*—that led me to the impression I was simply, to him, a tasty side of meat.

Maybe that's why he felt like I'd known him forever. Not him specifically, but his type? You better believe it.

His full lips tugged sideways, dark hair trimmed close, diamond flashing in one earlobe when he bowed his head to me. Still holding my hand. Possessively, power crawling over the contact.

And, *ew*.

When I'd first met Cooper Hudson, I'd worried. I knew handsome guys like him from my world. Had been surrounded by attractive and powerful young men my whole life, pretty much. Learned not to trust them, not really, since they were typically after power—my family's—or a simple and uncomplicated interaction—not that I was a prude, but one night stands weren't my favorite after some rather disappointing performances. Coop had surprised me with his genuine caring, compassion and kindness. Handsome or not, he was a truly sweet and gentle soul who wanted to do the right thing, no matter what.

Elias Gael? Yeah. Other end of the spectrum. To the point I almost eyerolled now that I'd pushed my hormones past the initial *holy crap, he's gorgeous*.

Because lurking back there, behind those incredible icy eyes? Was a hunter.

Just try to make me prey.

Silas spoke up, a welcome distraction this time. "I'm wondering if you've noticed any easing of your symptoms with the application of the spell I gave you."

How to tell him that was a big fat heck no? "I'm sorry," I said. "I don't think so. But thank you for trying."

Silas offered a little, sad sigh, shrug. "I will continue to offer assistance, my dear Phoebe, if you'll indulge an old druid."

So sweet of him, really. I reached out on impulse, squeezed his hand, saw the surprise in his eyes. Something else I couldn't read. "Thank you," I said. "It means a lot to me."

I didn't expect him to fall speechless. If simple gratitude did that, I could only imagine how little of it he received. How sad.

"Forgive me," I said, "but I didn't know you had a nephew." Time to satisfy my curiosity, though I instantly regretted the question. Elias leaned closer, the inquiry clearly triggering the suggestion of my interest, while I was just being nosy, thanks.

Bad luck, just freaking go away already.

"My dear, departed sister," Silas said with enough sorrow I figured his loss had to be recent, "Ganymede, left her poor, only son in my care when she passed." Elias's face flickered with an expression that wasn't quite grief, and close enough to disdain I liked him even less. "He's been studying abroad and only recently returned to us."

"If I'd known such beauty and grace awaited me here," the smarmy creature said, suggestive smile making me sigh inside, "I'd have come home sooner."

Maybe I could have tried to be patient and nice about it. Made an alternate choice, instead offering him a deadpan look in return so he'd dial it down a bit in the blatant flirting department.

Seemed to work, flickering disappointment in his eyes hiding enough irritation I was suddenly possessed with the desire to continue to knock him off the high horse he'd rode in on. I really wasn't a nice person sometimes.

"I understand you possess a truly unique power," Elias said then, leaning back, though his attempt at conversation went in my second least favorite direction. Forcing me to bite back a sigh of *here we go again*.

"Phoebe is able to alter the fate of those she chooses to assist," I heard Silas say when I struggled for words that wouldn't be rude, exactly, but might get the point across, at least.

"Luck," I managed to blurt while contemplating how polite I would have to be considering this was Silas's nephew and everything. "I give good luck."

Elias's smile widened at that. "I could use some," he said. Nodded to me again. "Maybe you'll be kind enough at some point to consider it."

If I had a dollar for everyone who asked...

"Unfortunately," Silas's somber tone helped somewhat, though the dramatics weren't entirely necessary, "she suffers the consequences, as with all power. The price that must be paid is a reversal of her own fortunes."

"Only for a day," I said.

"How remarkable." Elias reached with casual ease across my shoulder and, a moment later, offered me one of the champagne flutes he'd just liberated.

Slick. And frustratingly predictable.

Thank the Great Mother for bad luck. While it sucked most of the time, there were instances when it served me despite itself. Like the instant I reached out with reluctance to accept the drink—I was kind of thirsty—and a pair of laughing, rather drunk and disorderly young witches, their tuxedos in disarray and reeking of tobacco laced with whatever it was that made their cheeks flush and their pupils flare to fill their corneas, stumbled between us and spilled the offering before I could accept it.

Giving me the break I needed from discomfort of having to reject Elias—rude or not, it was going to happen and I wasn't looking forward to the outcome—while Silas and several others attempted to quiet the commotion. Hoping my luck would hold for at least a few seconds, I faded backward into the watching crowd and out of reach, finally turning to escape from the ballroom to the main foyer and out into the night for a breath of air.

Time to find a closet to hide in before anything else could happen.

By the time midnight came and the Yule ceremony unfolded, I'd succeeded in setting fire to the buffet table (don't ask), ruined someone's spellcasting by stumbling into the reach of their wand so they waved left instead of right, turning the potted plant in the line of fire into a ravening vine monster that took four druids to contain, made a little girl cry when I stepped on her doll and subsequently broke it trying to put it back to rights.

Among countless other, more minor issues that plagued me and drove me to the edge of frustrated desperation.

I could have cornered Selene, but she was busy with Jericho and I didn't want to interfere. Not to mention Elias seemed to be a friend of my sister's choice of partners, and the last thing I needed was more contact with Silas's predator nephew while my irritation amped and the need to smack him drove me to something epically disastrous. There was Mom, but she had become embroiled in a conversation with Dominion and Saraphella Richmond, the owners of the estate and our regal rulers as dual heads of the Academy of Adepts, over typical political matters that I preferred to stay out of.

That left Isolde, and no luck whatsoever, because my grandmother went missing about five seconds after we arrived, showed up for the ceremony looking rather mussed and her dress rumpled. Which had me cringing—not because she didn't deserve to have fun, but because I was not in the mood to listen to her talk about her latest exploits just to make me squirm.

Instead, fighting off tears at the sheer weight of my frustration, I hung back as the Richmonds dumped the ceremonial herb bundle into the flames of the main fire in the back garden, the flash of multi-hued light just for show, and hugged myself while everyone cheered and the party started up all over again.

Some ceremony. Grouch.

I turned to find somewhere to huddle and ran into a tray full of food, knocking it and the server sideways with a clash of silver platter on marble, and was done. Grabbed said servant by the front of his jacket and snarled in his face. "My besom and robe," I said.

Caught his jerking nod of surprise with enough fear behind it I pulled back, hating I'd been mean to someone who didn't deserve it, but reaped the reward when, a moment later, he returned in a matching flicker of light with my possessions.

I heard Selene calling my name and ignored her, sweeping on my robe and carrying my broom into open space, hopping on sidesaddle and whispering for it to rise. It did so, carrying me high above the house while I did look down, seeing my sister waving at me, then give up and turn away, leaving me to head for home on my own.

Where I would never, ever leave.

CHAPTER TEN

My ride home, while tiring and boring, was uneventful so my gratitude when I touched down on the roof of the brownstone knew no bounds. I paused a moment when I passed through the wards, feeling something hit me, almost like a rejection of the power that was my family's protections, and grunted at the impact.

That was all I needed. Tell me I didn't trigger a warning to Mom to come home early over nothing. But, whatever the trigger, the wards settled and then welcomed me as usual, likely due to the besom Isolde gifted me. I hugged my new broom, carrying it inside, sending giant thanks to my grandmother for it, trudging down the steps to the third floor and my room.

I didn't even shed my cloak or climb out of the silver dress, kicking off the sandals in the last bit of energy I had left, using the cowl as a pillow as I hit the mattress and snuggled under the heavy fur, darkness taking me.

The sound of my family returning woke me, disoriented and out of touch with time, sitting up abruptly and in surprise at their voices, their laughter, Mom clearly drunk and singing, Selene's giggles and my grandmother's deep chuckles a sign they were, at least, in excellent humor.

All the warning I had when my door burst open and the three came inside, carrying me along with them as they exited again and swept down the stairs in a refusal to accept no for an answer, their giddiness contagious and my collapsed nap sufficient to perk me up so I could appreciate their good humor.

"Mom made chocolate truffles," Selene whispered, eyes bright, lipstick gone, her carefully piled hair at an odd angle. Someone had fun, if the faint red mark on her neck was an indicator of Jericho Richmond's attentions. "Just for us."

Well now, that was reason for getting up in the middle of the night. And I wasn't being sarcastic either. Mom's chocolate truffles made eating anything else in life a pale, sad and pathetic attempt to recreate the awesome burst of smooth, buttery, melty cocoa deliciousness wrapped around a caramel creamy mint mass of heavenly interior I sometimes woke from dreams about.

I have no idea who stopped first, though I know I flashed from happy again and resigned to losing the rest of my night's sleep to *what the hecking feck* to *holy freaking no way* in about three heartbeats that felt a bit like a slow motion ticking of a second hand from one emotion to the next.

All I knew was, one instant my hearth was laughing, mostly drunk—me excepted—and without a care in the world. And the next? We stood as a foursome of stunned silence staring at the spread-eagled form of a young man in a hoody, face down on the carpet of the entry to our second floor living room.

"You were all out." Detective Morales had already taken in our clothing, the late hour, now well past 4AM and counting. It was clear we'd been to a party, wasn't it? Didn't that make her question a silly one?

"We were," Mom answered her, nodding, arms folded over her ample chest, face serious while she stared at me with worry and doubt in her blue eyes.

Because, if it was up to my mother? Detective Anna Morales and her partner, Detective Nathan Sallow, along with a forensics team in white coveralls and booties and blue latex gloves with cameras and all kinds of equipment and medical examiner, EMTs and pair of gaping uniforms wouldn't have taken over our living room under any circumstances.

The conversation had gone a little like this:

"I'll take care of the body." That had been Mom, after checking to be sure the young man in the ski mask—no it wasn't lost on me his description, though his body position made it impossible for me to check his lip for a scar.

"You can't, Mom." Yes, that had been me. "We have to call the police."

"You've cracked your cauldron, bratness." Isolde waved off my contribution.

"I don't know." Selene had stepped up, if hesitantly, shock and anxiety at war on her face. "Maybe Phoebe is right." She prodded him with the toe of one shoe. "He's normal, after all."

"How by the hearth of our ancestors did he even get in?" Mom spun in a circle, the wards flashing in response, runes hanging in the air, everything in place.

"An excellent question," my sister said, voice vibrating with the Maiden's power. "One that's our job to uncover. But murder?" She shook her head. "Mortal murder isn't for us to discard so callously." The Maiden had her own opinions, clearly. I had no doubt if Selene thought she could get away with it, she'd be on the side of the others, if not for her power's insistence. Instead, the Maiden chose my way of thinking. Her power visibly surfaced, reaching out to the body, joined by that of the Mother and the Crone, circling him in ribbons of light, snuffling and winding but unable to reach him for some reason.

"There's more at work here than we though," the Mother said. "We are blocked from investigating his end."

"Indeed," the Crone answered. "And, in case you missed it, his spirit is gone."

Right. The wards would have caught it, kept it here long enough to question it. Should have. Hadn't?

The Maiden sighed. "Our magic won't work to uncover his death." The three ribbons rose, twined together. Selene's defeated tone deciding our next action. "If we want to find out what happened, we need help unconnected to our wards."

"If we care," the Crone said. "Do we?"

"Perhaps we should," the Mother answered. "If this was an attack, it may only be the beginning. I, for one, would like to know."

"We could contact the Academy," the Maiden said.

But it was Mom who shook her head, surfacing from the great power inside her. She turned to me. "More mundane investigation may be all we need to uncover the truth and keep others out of it. Especially if, somehow, this human managed to find a way past our wards on his own." Murmured agreement from Selene, but a glare from Isolde. "It shouldn't be possible. But, before we inquire in our world, let's find out what his world has to say." My sister nodded, Isolde tsking her disapproval. And Mom finally addressed me, though she'd been looking at me the whole time. "Your friends at the police department," she said then. "Will they come?"

That had been, it turned out, a rather silly

question.

My hurried text to Morales had her and Sallow at our door in under ten minutes, both of them rumpled and recently roused from bed, a pair of uniforms behind them and the forensics team with the medical examiner and EMTs following a few minutes later.

Things hadn't been as jovial between us as I'd hoped. Didn't help my grandmother sat in a wingback with an irritated expression and waved off any attempt the detectives made to ask her questions, pointedly telling me as though they weren't even there, "I'm not taking part in this ridiculous extravagance, disobedient child, so you can see it through."

I tried to focus on Morales, finally piping up as an afterthought. "They were at the party until 3:30 or so," I said, "but I came home early, shortly after 1AM."

Mom hissed in a breath, glared at me. While the medical examiner looked up from his preliminary check of the body, liver thermometer still in hand.

"Shortly after time of death. I'm putting it at 12:30." Dr. Ian Percy had no qualms, it seemed, pinning me with his kind of helpful. Not to mention the fact he met my eyes behind his round glasses with judgment showing loud and clear. Our brief intro on his arrival had been brusque but professional. Now? Yeah, it was pretty obvious he saw me in a new light.

Morales made a note, her own expression grim.

"You didn't hear or see anything when you got home? Even though you came in after the victim died?"

How could I tell her I wasn't downstairs, that I'd flown in on a broom, not come in the normal way? "It was dark," I said, knowing how weak that sounded and that my bad luck wasn't doing me any favors and did I really just turn into the prime suspect?

"He's wearing a hoody and a mask," I blurted. "Like the homeless sketch today."

Morales didn't waver, didn't nod, left me to hang myself. Which I did, because I had no filter at the moment, it seemed, and was unable to stop myself from digging a hole big enough for my own coffin. "I saw him earlier. Or someone dressed like him. At the end of the alley." I pointed in the vague direction, watched myself, as if from outside my body, as I stumbled and fumbled through delivering information in the herky-jerky method of a drug addict coming down from a bad hit. "Smoking, hanging around. He saw me and left. I didn't go after him because I'm not a detective." Oh dear.

Oh dear, oh dear. Just stop talking.

Morales cut me a bit of slack, not cuffing me at least, though, to my surprise, it was Sallow who snorted, brushing a few crumbs from the front of his golf shirt he'd gained by sampling the cookie tray Mom hastily offered the gathering because she couldn't help herself. "You just described the uniform of petty thieves and crack dealers, kid," he said. "Come on, Morales, you really liking Phoebe for this?"

I could have kissed him while the tall detective sighed and shrugged.

"I'll have more questions once the forensics team is done," she said.

"Dr. Percy." I glanced across to the slim young woman crouched next to her boss, whose dark eyes met mine a moment before she returned to her job. The medical examiner's assistant, as it turned out to my shock and slight hope my luck might not be all bad, was none other than Mirabelle Whitehall, not just a fellow witch but an old friend. "I'm finding no visible signs of cause of death." Another glance.

A message.

That the young man—or thief or whoever he was—wasn't just normal but had likely been killed by magical means.

Excellent. I was, however, more interested to know how he'd gotten past our protections in the first place. Was he here simply to steal from us, had, perhaps through my bad luck, found a way in? Got caught in the wards and died?

That felt incredibly unlikely for some reason. The only other option? Someone sent him. Someone from our world. And gave him the means to bypass our protections, through a faulty means, clearly.

So, who sent him here? Or was it just a stupid round of luck and I was to blame for a string of coincidences that led to the unfortunate end of a plain and simple thief?

In probably the worst timing ever, two things happened. The front door, now open to normals thanks to Mom allowing them to pass the wards to let the police in, filled with the tall, worried form of Officer Cooper Hudson. Who started toward me at the same instant he was shouldered aside by the arrival of Jericho Richmond, Silas Gael and, to the absolute credit of my terrible fortunes, Elias.

Because that was just the very worst combination of conflicting coming togethers in the face of a murder accusation that could possibly culminate at my feet.

CHAPTER ELEVEN

I faded back out of the reach of the detectives and Jericho took over, Silas behind him, Elias instantly crossing the room to join me. Something Coop instantly noticed. I had the towering handsome cop at my side, not touching me but looming protectively, while the younger Gael ignored him, taking my hand, all before Jericho could speak.

While that weird familiar feeling of Elias woke again, making me shiver and, instead of pull away immediately as I'd planned to do, pause. Stare. What was that between us, anyway? Only to realize my hesitation? Wasn't lost on Coop.

Well, that was a wonderful turn of events. The last thing I needed was a head-butting ego war in the middle of this mess.

Took my hand back finally though, thanks.

"Jericho Richmond," he offered his card to Morales. "My father's firm represents the Monday family. I would advise you, officers, not to speak to any of them further without myself or one of our lawyers present."

"Detectives," Morales growled, handing the card off to Sallow who shrugged and tucked it in his pocket. "We were just finishing up here, Mr. Richmond."

"Excellent news. Make sure you don't repeat the mistake, *officer*." Yup, he used that word again on purpose, calculated to piss her off. So easy to read on his handsome face, to see it trigger her despite herself, because the Morales I'd been getting to know was an Amazonian princess under fire, queen of poise and sarcasm. But I'd never seen the full wattage of Jericho's arrogance before, though I suppose I'd had rare opportunities to even interact with Jericho or his cronies aside from my times with Selene. Sure, there were rumors about his penchant for bullying, but I'd always given him the benefit of the doubt because I guess I just never associated that sort of behavior with him. The way he treated Morales, however? Woke a surprising snarl of protectiveness inside me, how he looked down his nose like she wasn't worth his time. Sure, some of our kind treated humans like they weren't as good as us, but I'd never witnessed it.

Until now.

Or maybe it was just his breeding, the fact he'd grown up in privilege. Well, so had I, thanks, and it didn't turn me into a jackass.

Dr. Percy interrupted with an abrupt, "Excuse

us," the EMTs pushing the gurney with the body bagged dead guy between Jericho and Anna, breaking the moment of growing tension that I was sure the young Richmond intended, cold smile cruel. Suddenly, he wasn't so handsome anymore.

"Detective Morales," I said, stepping forward, partially to exit the influence of the still lingering Elias but mostly because this was Anna we were talking about. "Anything you need. Please, we just want to know what happened." She softened a little, though her amber eyes were wary and I couldn't help but feel hurt by that. "Do you still need me to come in and sketch for you today?" Yikes, it was almost dawn.

Her hesitation hurt more than her denial. "Let's hold off," she said, walking past me, Sallow eye rolling behind her back before squeezing my shoulder. "We'll be in touch."

And, just like that, the crowd in our living room shrank to my family, Jericho and company and, to my surprise, the still lingering Coop.

I turned, looked up at him, noticed Elias had crowded my space all over again when I wasn't looking. Opened my mouth to say something while the young druid casually draped his arm over my shoulder. Like he owned me. Stiffened at the contact, but worse, at the flicker of hurt in Coop's eyes.

No, it wasn't like that. Why couldn't I say so?

Even as Anna poked her head inside.

"Officer Hudson." No ifs or buts in that tone of voice.

"Coming, ma'am." He didn't say anything about Elias, just offered me a brave smile and a nod, failing at masking his clear heartbreak, taking the suggestion my unwelcome companion offered in that simple gesture of possessiveness while I spluttered internally, lips locked in the silence bad luck wrapped around me as firmly as the contact with Elias. Coop took the time to wave to my mother, sister and grandmother, bypassing the magical self-assigned cavalry and headed out the door.

"Now," Jericho said, spinning to frown at my mother. "Tell us what happened and spare no details."

With Coop gone, my bad luck shifted and I was finally able to shake off Elias' touch, scowling up at him.

"Don't do that again," I snapped.

He backed off a half step, icy eyes wide in mock apology, hands up. "Just trying to help," he said.

Liar.

Nothing to be done for it until I could talk to Coop. I hated he'd jumped to the obvious conclusion, though, naturally, I hadn't been able to reassure him because this just had to turn out to be the worst day of my life. Though, as I sank to the sofa with my hands tucked between my knees, weary all over again, while Mom filled Jericho in on what we'd uncovered, I did finally accept the truth staring me in the heart.

Coop meant a lot to me. Like, boyfriend material. And I had to either accept that and do something about it, or let him go.

Elias, for his part, now that he'd ruined everything, rejoined his uncle. And it was Silas who dug into the earth with his druidic power, recreating the death scene in perfect 3D model, the image holding while Mom finished her retelling.

"Where," Jericho said, looking around, "is the human's spirit?"

He didn't wait for anyone to answer, his own power rippling outward, sorcery dropping the whole room into dimness while he tapped into the electrical system. Despite his demand and the thrumming focus of his summons, augmented by the city's power grid, no spirit appeared. Something else much more troubling did, however.

Because as he called to the soul of the young man who'd died in our house, he instead triggered our wards. Only, they weren't the bright and sparkling Moon washed silvery perfection I was used to. Instead, dull and thrumming with effort, they surfaced under Jericho's touch, a dirty shadow passing over them.

Drawing a deep gasp from the throats of the triunity of my family.

"We have a serious problem," Jericho said then, stern expression not rousing even a little comfort. While Silas nodded, his own long, lean face paled out to ash.

"My dears," he said, "I'm afraid your wards are compromised."

"Tainted," Jericho said, lips twisting in disgust.

He appeared almost near revulsion, gaze sliding over Selene as though regretting their association now. The pig.

"Who has done this?" Isolde stood, lashing them with her words, and even the arrogance Jericho seemed to use like a weapon when he decided we weren't worthy vanished in the wake of her displeasure. Something akin to fear woke behind his eyes and he actually backed off, letting Silas handle my grandmother.

As if anyone could.

"Be assured," her friend said, that deep regret unwavering, "we shall uncover that truth, Isolde. But, for now, I beg you all. Seek for yourself and tell me why it is they feel like you and you alone?"

Isolde tsked, reached for Mom's hand, Selene's, as the powers of the Great Mother coursed through them, the triunity of the sacred feminine gathering like a small sun in the circle they made before bursting outward in a ring of light.

Impacting the wards.

Rebounding when they struck the familiar symbols hanging in the air, no longer bright white and gold and pink or blue, but again appearing sullied, their colors dimmed, the shadow of something interfering with the power of the hearth weighing on the wards.

"Impossible," grandmother said, breathless. "Source!" She dove in again, Mom and Selene straining with her. Another ball of light, another burst of power. This time, their attempt won, pushing whatever it was back, but not eliminating it entirely.

If anything, the shadow only shifted, realigned, settling deeper into the wards while my family sagged from the effort.

A task that should have been effortless.

"This is tied to whatever happened to the man you found." Silas shook his head, large hands spreading wide. "I'm so sorry, my dears. We will work tirelessly to uncover the truth. But the fact remains, either this has been an existing problem," no way, never, impossible, "or his death has tainted your protections. Which can only happen for one reason."

He did *not* just go there.

Because the number one cause of taint in personal power? Could only happen if we'd built the wards on death.

Which was, naturally, illegal and disgusting and revolting and there was no way anyone would ever believe it of us. Not our hearth. Not the Monday family, one of the most revered, sacred, the bearers of the wonderworks, blessed by the Great Mother Moon herself?

Except the look on Jericho's face, the regret in Silas's? The horror that crawled over my grandmother like a living thing? Only Elias seemed unconcerned by the reveal, arms crossed over his chest, still in his tuxedo I realized in an absent aside, as was Jericho, observing in curiosity and silence.

CHAPTER TWELVE

I escaped to my room, though no one noticed, contemplating sleep but knowing it wouldn't be coming anytime soon. Ended up dozing in and out for hours, feeling in the way of the three women I loved more than anything who locked themselves in their triunity to tackle the wards.

The moment of release from my bad luck? Felt like a hug, the tension of it easing in an exhale that relaxed my entire body and, sighing out the last of the awful that held me, I finally felt ready to face the world.

Showered and dressed, I emerged hopefully at last, only to find they were still fighting off the taint. Knowing I couldn't help and would likely only hinder, I chose to get out of the house or lose my mind.

The walk home refreshed me, was even pleasant, the evening cool but not icy cold, fresh snow just starting to fall when I finished my hour-long exercise, reaching my block with optimism renewed. We were Mondays. My family would figure this out and life would go back to normal. Maybe I was lying to myself, but the ease of tension never felt so good and I embraced the shift in my luck like never before. No, I didn't regret helping Unk Jay-Jay and this experience wouldn't stop me from doing what I could for the next poor soul who needed me. And.

Phew, baby.

Speaking of luck, guess who I spotted at the far end of my alley, digging around in the dumpster outside the shop exit? A grin split my face, my hand rising, already planning to run inside and grab him some of Mom's amazing food and maybe some fresh socks, but before I could flag down Unk or even let him know I was there, the whole world screeched to a stop.

As a black van, windowless and driven by a person in a mask and hoodie, did the same right next to the old man.

The door slid open and a second hooded figure leaped out. Grabbed Unk.

I was moving, though I hadn't known I'd started to run, made it to the end of the alley only because Unk fought his attacker, managed to pull partially free, his eyes locking on mine, shouting in fear as the man in the mask struck him on the back of the head with what looked like a brick.

Unk fell, forcing the assailant to heave him bodily toward the van. Giving me time to lunge and grab him, without thinking because, let's be honest, five foot one and a hundred scrawny pounds against someone desperate enough to kidnap a helpless homeless man?

Not great odds.

I had no magic to help, only my person to try to stop the crime. Felt my hand slide over the back of the hoodie, but make no purchase, the kidnapper rolling sideways with Unk into the van while I hit my knees in the icy slush and stared up as the door slammed in my face.

The van peeled out before I could do anything else.

Looked like I'd come out of the power too soon to do him any good.

Unk's luck had run out.

It took me a moment to regain my feet, boots sliding in the wet slush, though it was obvious from the prodding flickers of memory the man in the mask who'd kidnapped Unk was no other than the same one who'd robbed him just yesterday. Part of my imbalance came from being thrown against the moment in time I'd lived inside the homeless man's head. When I finally did regain my stability, I took a breath to calm my racing heart, already knowing what I was going to do.

I rubbed my fingertips together, the part of me that touched the kidnapper warming a little when I did, sparks of faint yellow falling from my hand to the ground. Lighting up the place he'd fallen, his body's impact leaving a trace behind I could tap into, leading to a footprint where his shoe landed before he rolled into the van.

Obviously the trail ended there. Without physical contact with the earth it became harder to trace him through the law of contagion I triggered. Just a little spellworking, nothing major, more a parlor trick than anything. Still as benign as it was, the connection between two physical things could be used to advantage and I had every intent of doing so.

Because despite what Detective Sallow said about uniforms of the criminal and cowardly? The man who'd taken Unk was rather a bit too similar to the one we'd found dead in my living room. And finding him here, so close to home, only increased my discomfort. I'd never seen Unk around my house in the past, though that didn't mean much, I admitted to myself. I, like most people, had a bit of a blind spot when it came to the disenfranchised and displaced. Maybe guilt was part of my reasoning, though much more so it came from the now personal link I felt I shared with the old man.

If I could use what power I had to track him down, I would. And perhaps solve the murder at the same time.

I inhaled, closed my eyes, let my internal vision take over. While the power of air could be less reliable, the spell I'd cast would linger until it cleansed from the subject. If I got on it fast enough, didn't let the movement of air dispel his path, there was a possibility I could find the kidnapper.

Luck, it seemed, was on my side more than usual,

the floating yellow specks visible to my internal sight. After a hesitant moment considering calling the police, I finally shook my head. How would I explain knowing where they'd gone? If I involved normal cops, even the ones I worked with, they would take too long to get here. I had minutes, if that, to track the path to wherever they'd taken Unk. I could follow, find him then call Coop or Morales and hopefully hand over the poor homeless man while possibly solving the crime I seemed to be a suspect in.

Maybe Morales was wearing off on me, but I found my boots carrying me onward despite my trepidation and reassurance I'd do nothing on the other end but make a call and hurried off into the softly snowing evening.

The fact they could have driven off into the countryside and this whole exercise was one in futility wasn't lost on me. Still, I'd made my choice and that stubborn streak I'd earned from my grandmother wasn't going to let me stop unless I had to. I was crossing my fourth intersection and considering attempting a besom call—would my new broom come to me if I asked? It just might—to take to the air for the duration when the sparking wisps of light I followed thickened. As though my target had stopped.

Except, instead of leading to footprints or possible exits, they simply pooled and that was that. I stood outside a large, brick building in the more industrial side of town, enough traffic I felt safe, at least, though me randomly following kidnappers and then standing around like an idiot looking for them might not have been the wisest choice.

I was six blocks from the precinct. Made another decision when there was no obvious place to search further without putting myself in danger and headed for the police station.

Morales seemed surprised to see me, but welcomed me when I entered the bullpen, waving me toward her desk. Sallow looked up from his jelly donut, powder on the brown reindeer tie he wore, waving like nothing was wrong. I joined them both, hesitant but knowing I had to say something, when the beautiful detective pointed at my wet, dirty knees with a frown.

"You okay?" Those amber eyes had enough concern I knew no matter what happened, this was the right choice.

I told them both what I'd seen, what happened, caught the eyebrow arch from Morales, the hum of ooh boy from Sallow when I confessed to trying to stop the kidnappers.

When I was done, pausing as I thought about if I should share that I'd followed, Morales pulled out a chair and sat me in it, intense expression on high alert.

"Again," she said. "Slowly this time." I had a penchant for talking fast, I admit it, when I wasn't feeling comfortable. This time, after a deep inhale and exhale, feeling a hand settle on my shoulder, I relaxed fully, smiling at Coop who joined us with his own kind expression shifting to the detective a moment.

Morales just shrugged.

And I went through it again, in as much detail as I could. "I'm positive it's the same man who robbed Unk," I said. How could I know that? "The description was a perfect match." Sallow's excuses about criminal choices in attire aside.

That very detective grunted at Anna, setting aside his donut remnants as though he'd forgotten his own excuse to the contrary. "That's four," he said.

Wait, what did he say? "You mentioned others," I said, "that you wanted me to sketch some attackers. Was it the same man?"

Morales didn't respond right away, sitting back to cross her arms over her chest, staring at the floor with a deep frown. It was Coop who filled me in, softly and with some hesitation but braver when his superiors didn't tell him to stop.

"There's been a series of attacks on homeless people in the last week," he said. "Thing is, there could be more because they don't always report. But we have been hearing the ones that do? Disappear shortly after. This just confirms it." One more glance at Morales who was nodding, grim, angry.

"Thank you, Phoebe," she said, standing abruptly. "This helps. Though I don't suppose you have a license number?"

I shook my head, mind spinning over scenarios, lame excuse after pathetic attempt to come up with some safe way to tell her about the brick building where the sparkles had come to a pooling stop making indecision an agony. I had to act, and yet, I couldn't put my family at further risk. They had to come first and if I somehow managed to stir the magic user pot further trying to help... yes. That would be just my luck.

I finally shrugged inside my puffy coat, knees aching from the fall, feeling dirty and damp and wanting a hot bath. I'd done what I could, hoped Unk would be okay, happy to hear the officers I thought of as friends cared. They were the police. They could handle it, right?

Guilt sucked so much.

I stood then, turned to go while the two detectives whispered a moment, before Anna stopped me, hand on my arm.

"Look, kid," she said, "we know you didn't kill that guy, okay? And your family's story checks out. I'm sorry about how things went."

Not hard to instantly deny her apology. "You were doing your job," I said. "Thanks for coming so fast when I called."

That earned me one of her rare smiles. "Of course," she said.

"Do you know what happened to him? How he died?" Would be helpful to know, maybe. If the wards ended up killing him, damaged as they were, that could be very bad. But if it was some more mundane reason, at least I could offer my family that comfort.

Anna shook her head then. "Nothing from the

ME yet," she said. Glanced at Coop who hovered close enough I could smell him. Yum. "Why don't we have Officer Hudson give you a ride home. You've had a hell of a day."

"My pleasure," Coop blurted while I nodded, despite the uncomfortable moment with Elias. I was just as happy to accept. The idea of walking home at the moment really didn't appeal to me. And, having the chance to talk to Coop now that my luck had turned? Absolute necessity.

A few minutes later, warm in the front seat of his cruiser, I found myself watching a homeless woman on the corner as we drove by. Which, naturally, led to thoughts of Unk Jay-Jay and the other victims, heart aching as much as my knees. "I wish there was something I could do." Careful, witch girl. I knew better than to put emotion behind needs like that. And yet, it was hard not to want to help.

Coop reached over and squeezed my hand in his big, warm one. "You were amazing coming in like that," he said. "So many people just don't want to get involved. And the homeless don't like to tell us anything. They don't trust us."

"You have a tough job," I said, squeezing back. "Thanks for being so kind, Coop."

Made him blush. There was a nice change. And a perfect segue moment.

Except, it was Coop who got to the point first. When he pulled up in front of the brownstone, the snow had stopped but the ground was slushy enough I found myself being told to wait in my seat until he got out, circled the car, and assisted me to the sidewalk.

"I didn't know you were seeing someone." He sounded like he'd worked out what he was going to tell me in his head, the statement apologetic and rushed. "If I had, Phoebe, I swear I wouldn't have been just a jackass." Oh, no. I had to steer this ship off the rocks, except he wasn't giving me time to fix it, hurrying on, smiling in a wry and adorable way that broke my heart. "You know I think you're amazing. And I'm happy to have you as a friend, no matter what." He looked away then, while I fishlipped and sagged inside my coat. Had I lost the chance I'd only just realized I really wanted? "I promise I'll find out what's going on," he said, expression darkening while he tucked his hands into the pockets of his jacket. "I hate that you were involved, Phoebe. I worry about you and your family." He glanced down the alley, and I knew he was about to suggest walking me right to my door.

One hand on his arm stopped that in its tracks, while I fought for words to tell him how wrong he was. And finally sighed over the mess. Decided to think things through first. So I didn't make an even bigger disaster of things. Because right now, my mind was tired, my heart hurt and I just wasn't sure I would say what I needed to. Instead, I let him see how much I appreciated him, hoped it translated on my face. "I'm okay," I said. "Honest. Thanks again."

He waved as I walked away, and I waved back, knowing he watched me the entire way despite what he'd just said. Second-guessed about a million times that short walk, about running back and telling him Elias was nothing, had done that on some creepy purpose of his own, that I really, truly had feelings for the handsome officer I left behind.

Because I didn't act on that push and pull, instead finally reaching the entry and jerking the door open and ducked inside.

Safe. Sigh. And probably for the best. My family would eat him alive.

I didn't have a chance to move from that spot. My mother's voice reached me and the message hit loud and clear.

Phoebe, she sent. *We're in trouble. Don't come home.*

CHAPTER THIRTEEN

Hard not to come to a complete and utter halt when your mother shared something so dire. However, my instant desire to rush to help decided to have a short and rather terse argument with my ingrained training to listen to the woman who raised me.

What can I do? Surprising, how calm I sounded in my own head.

Silas is here, Mom sent, sounding rather collected herself, a sure sign she was ready to blow. My mother's enthusiasm for life and emotion rarely hid behind anything which could only mean she was on the edge of her temper. *It's been confirmed. The wards are terminally tainted.* That was terrible news. If they couldn't be cleared, it meant tearing them down completely, starting again. Which might not sound like a big deal. Except, those wards had been built from the ground up and added to by each and every

Monday witch who had ever been. Erasing them would take all the power my family had. Building them again? I couldn't even imagine the years it would take. Leaving us vulnerable in the interim and likely at the mercy of the Academy for protection.

I held my breath thinking about how Isolde took that news.

Mom wasn't done. *We've been officially notified the Academy of Adepts plans to investigate and, if charges are warranted, we will be banished at the least.*

And the worst? I knew better than to ask.

The fire, she sent as though that weren't even an issue.

Mom. I swallowed past the sting of tears, the tightening in my throat. *Someone has to be behind this.*

We are of that mind as well, the Mother sent, before she retreated and Mom returned. *Clearly, we have been targeted, that much is obvious. But finding out who had decided to attack our family may not be easily uncovered.* This couldn't be happening. We were one of the most revered families in the Academy. My mind spluttered over the audacity, the unbelievability of such an act while Mom paused. *Are you still friends with Mirabelle Whitehall?*

As a matter of fact. I leaned into the wall near the door, breathing through my mouth and staring at my boots to keep from running upstairs. *As far as I know*, I sent.

She's named as the medical investigator, Mom sent. *I need you to talk to her, Phoebe. Find out what evidence they have against us.*

This is ridiculous, I sent back.

Clearly. Her calm helped, despite the fact I knew it meant trouble. *Darling dear, just do as I ask, please. We'll hold things together here. But I need you to stay out of it. Do you understand?*

While my family was thrown under the bus by who knew what conspiracy? Because there was no way they'd even dabbled in blood rituals without me knowing it.

Despite the utter ridiculousness of it, I had to accept someone was trying to destroy us. Sure, maybe I was spending too much time in the company of cops, but I was positive if I laid out the real case to Morales and Sallow, to Coop? A set-up would be the first thing they'd suggest, too.

I won't abandon you, Mom, I sent. *I'll go see Mirabelle right now.*

Phoebe. That was my grandmother, the weight of her mind and the Crone's in my head. *You are to remain outside this, child. If our family is to survive, promise us you will do as you are asked. Only we three are named. It will stay that way.*

BeeBee, please. Selene had to poke her nose in. *I can bear anything if I know you're safe.*

How could they ask me to just let them go to the fire if it came to that?

I'm going to find out what happened, I sent then, shutting them all down. *No way is anyone taking my family from me.*

Be careful, my pet, Mom sent.

Stubborn bratness, Isolde sent. *I have every faith in you.*

Love you, Beebs. And then, the three were gone and I was alone in the entry, panting my growing anger and terror into the quiet of the downstairs darkness.

I would save them. Or die trying.

First things first. I'd known Mirabelle my whole life, and seeing her last night gave me a refreshed contact. Easy enough to exit the doorway into the cold evening and reach out to her, through the old connection, locating her, not at home, but the morgue.

Perfect.

The cab I hired dropped me at the hospital, the side doorway to the morgue easy enough to find. Though, the security guard just inside took notice at my entry, something I hadn't considered.

"Hi," I said, going for perky and confident. "I'm the sketch artist for Detectives Morales and Sallow. They asked me to compare what I drew to the body they brought in for the Monday case." Bald-faced lying was not my forte, the slow blush creeping up my neck and across my chest about to turn me in when it hit my cheeks.

But this was for my family. No way was I going to let them down.

The guard just grunted, waving me on and, to my surprise and a release of hysterical giggles behind both mittened hands, I found myself hurrying down the hall on the other side of the swinging doors.

Easy enough to follow the faint trail to Mirabelle, stronger as I neared the end of the wide corridor. The powerful scent of disinfectant and death slowed my pace, until I stood a long moment at the swinging metal entry to the morgue. The two round, glass windows showed my target bending over a body on a stainless steel slab, bright lights shining on her dark corkscrew curls, making her deep mahogany skin glow. She looked up before I could enter, sensing me, I suppose, face almost obscured by the light shining on the clear plastic mask she wore.

There was a long moment of hesitation before she waved with one gloved hand for me to enter. I did, though the lingering taint of death gave me instant goosebumps. Sometimes I hated being a chicken.

"I suppose I should have expected you to show up." Mirabelle pushed back the face shield, frown pulling her face into a disapproving and rather mature expression more suited to someone older than her. She was, after all, my age, only twenty-four, but somehow felt like my elder. "I can't talk to you, Phoebe. Academy of Adepts orders." She turned away from me again, looking down at the dead man on her slab. "You wasted a trip, I'm afraid. Now, if you don't mind, I have work to do and evidence to collect for my superiors."

"You sound like you've already decided my family is guilty." There was a time I might have backed down and just left. I hadn't expected her to embrace me with open arms, though we had been dear friends when we were girls together. But this almost accusatory tone of voice, the arrogance and judgment in the way she dismissed me? I wasn't known for my temper, but I had one. And about as much judgment of my own to hand out when the time was right.

She looked up again, angry despite herself. The coldness she'd begun with wasn't going to last, that was obvious. "Then how do you explain the evidence against them, Phoebe?" Mirabelle tossed her head, massive curls barely contained in the kerchief she wore. "Is this how your hearth has built their power? Many speculate, you know, how the Monday family manages to maintain such control over the wonderworks when none others are able."

How *dare* she?

"Sounds like someone's been eating sour grapes," I snapped back. "Considering my family has held the wonderworks for centuries and this has never, ever been an issue, I would think we would be granted the benefit of the doubt instead of instant shame and accusation. Because, surely no one has a grudge against us or desire to claim the wonderworks for themselves." That was it, wasn't it? The thing I struggled to accept. That one of our own, or a group for all I knew, longed for possession of that which my family had been gifted by the Great Mother so long ago. "Nice to know you and all the other powers I know are that petty and jealous of the magic my family controls you're willing to toss aside any thread of solidarity and, instead, decide we're guilty."

That got through to her, Mirabelle's anger fading, faint guilt passing through the aura around her. If she knew she wasn't in full control of herself, she'd have been horrified, though I kept her slip to myself.

"I just want to know what happened," I said, taking a few steps forward, softening my tone. "My family is innocent, Mirabelle, and no matter what you or the others might think, I will not let them go to the fire if someone is deliberately trying to harm us."

"I'm sorry." She sagged a little, shaking her head. "Phoebe, I didn't want to believe it, I swear. It's just... I've felt the tainted wards. I was there this morning."

"So was I," I said, "and that's the first time in my entire life I've felt what happened to our family's protections. Whoever tampered with them did so to hurt us. I think you just gave us the why, didn't you?" She flinched at that. "I'm going to find out who, Mirabelle, and I would appreciate at least a sliver of doubt in our favor. I think we've earned that."

She set aside her face mask, nodded to me. "That's fair," she said, "though I'll have to tell the Academy of Adepts I allowed you to see the body."

"As is proper," I said. "Both sides are required equal access to all evidence, especially in an accused crime this serious." I knew that much, at least.

Mirabelle's expression settled, as though I'd given her what she needed to confidently stand by her own decision. Made me angry, in a way. I had no idea she was such a coward, though I suppose standing up for others wasn't a virtue for some.

I stepped in, looked down, ignoring her now as I examined the young man on the slab. She had, as yet, to cut into him, thankfully, his pale face in repose, whitened corneas staring at the ceiling. But, it was the scar on his lip that caught my breath, the tug of it that pulled his mouth askew that had me blinking in disbelief.

"I know this man," I said. Shook my head when Mirabelle's frown returned. "Not personally. He attacked a homeless guy, stole from him. I did a sketch of him for the police two days ago." That triggered surprise on her face, in my own mind, despite the fact I'd already suggested this truth to Morales and Sallow. Hated I was right. Because it triggered a lot of unhappy questions around me and the power I wielded—controlled was by far the wrong word in my case. So, what was the thief doing in my house? Did he know of my connection to Unk Jay-Jay somehow? Had to have, since this was the homeless man's attacker, no doubt. Okay, time for the hard question. Was this whole disaster my fault? Considering I'd been in the middle of a bad luck cycle, that was possible and literally broke my heart.

Fortunately for me, the scar wasn't the only thing about him I discerned as the terror I'd led my family to disaster wormed its way into my soul. There was a flicker around him, like a faint shadow. His aura was gone, of course, though his spirit wasn't here, either, making me wonder yet again where it had gone. The biggest ah-ha, however, came from seeing through the flicker. To the truth.

Someone had created a glamor, and a very good one, only visible to me, I suppose, because I was looking closely.

"Mirabelle," I said, I leaned in closer, to be certain, and felt my second shock. "do you see that?" She shook her head, then inhaled with a breath of surprise, dark eyes huge. "Someone's tampered with him," I said.

She met my gaze with her own full of sudden doubt. "He's not human," she said. "He's one of us."

Which explained how he was able to break into our house. "So the supposition the wards killed him and stole his blood to feed the ritual is no longer valid," I said. "Only human blood is viable for rituals, is that right?"

She nodded slowly. "And animal," she said, "though the penalty for animal sacrifice is much smaller. What possible reason would someone have to disguise him as human? And," Mirabelle spun away, pacing a bit, hands tucked behind her back as she scowled at the floor, mind clearly working, "why send him into your home the night of Yule, knowing you'd be out?"

"To set us up," I said.

Mirabelle stopped, turned to me. Then rushed to hug me, cheek pressed to mine.

"Phoebe," she whispered. "I'm so sorry." When she let me go, her eyes had narrowed, full lips a thin line. "I'll log all the evidence and send it to the Academy of Adepts," she said. "Whatever else I find out, I'll let you know, I promise. Despicable, this act against your family. I should have known better than to listen to the petty jealousies of others."

At least I found an ally, one who could influence

the outcome of the case against my family. "Thanks, Mirabelle," I said. And left, my mind lit up with possibilities while that lingering anger remained, burning inside me.

I would find who tried to hurt my family, and why. And when I was done, they'd be the ones in the fire.

Sure, I might have been the least of us, but.

Don't mess with a Monday.

CHAPTER FOURTEEN

I took a cab home despite Mom's earlier orders to stay clear. Where else did I have to go? And besides, I needed to tell my family what was going on. The fact I was unable to reach them through magic generated a rush of worry that had me tossing concerns over my mother's disapproval to the wind.

There was a brief moment, as my cab passed the precinct, I considered heading to the police station to talk to the detectives. Who, of course, wouldn't be there after hours. I hesitated over calling Morales again, thought of Coop, discarded that idea, too. Was home and out of the cab, standing in our back alley, frozen in indecision and the chill of the evening, contemplating my next step before I could make a decision.

For all my bravado and smack talk? I was kind of at a loss for what to do next.

When I spotted the older woman pushing a baby

carriage piled with junk standing near my dumpster, I paused. Realized as she stood there she was staring at me and, on impulse, hurried toward her. Only to have her spin and rush away, the wheels of her carriage squeaking as she went.

Easy enough to follow her. The fact she was clearly homeless couldn't have been a coincidence, either. Did she know about my work with the police? Perhaps had something to tell me about Unk Jay-Jay and the other missing displaced? I sampled the air for the golden sparkles, caught a few traces of the kidnapper, but not enough to make me worry. If he was lurking around this woman, either he'd done so days ago or the bits and wisps I was seeing were merely coincidental.

My quarry moved surprisingly quickly for a hunched and elderly woman and it wasn't until she stopped at last I was able to catch her.

The small vacant lot where she'd set up her cardboard box house seemed to be part of a group squat with a few dirty tents and other flimsy constructions serving as living quarters for the handful of homeless who watched me when I approached with flat and unwelcoming expressions. I did my best to look innocent, smiling and nodding at those who glared at my passing, and kept my focus on the old woman who finally turned to look up into my eyes.

Only then did she let me see who she really was and, with another jolt of shock—hadn't I had enough for the last forty-eight hours?—I realized she wasn't human.

"Where is your hearth?" Empathy flooded even the well of anger I clung to, as I reached for her with power and my hand.

She batted my touch away in both regards, the magic within her weak but viable. Deep wrinkles had taken over her face, the gap-toothed grin she shot me crinkling her pale eyes to near slits, deeply set into her round, apple face. The heavy scarf and jacket she wore draped her in similar shape, making her look round all over, the knitted hat on her head bobbing with a large pompom when she bowed her head to me.

"All gone now," she said. "Only Mad Martie left." She cackled a sad little laugh before holding up both hands, showing me the aura that remained to her, faintly pink and soft, the trace of a hearth based in water and fire, likely a minor family with healing abilities leaving her as the last heir. "Still got it," she said, winking.

"You do." I smiled at her while an ache took the place of everything that came before. How had one of ours ended up discarded so callously? She was a witch, no matter her hearth circumstance. Another family should have taken her in, were obligated, as far as I was concerned. The fact I kind of had a thing for saving people and animals and things wasn't lost on me when I offered her my hand, slipping out of my mitten so she could see the rainbow of light that was my family's power. "Well met and welcome, sister."

She touched my palm with tentative hesitation,

sighing when the magics connected a moment. "Monday," she whispered, gaze soft.

I nodded then. "Yes," I said. "My family."

Mad Martie's eyes snapped open wide. "Trouble comes," she said. "Found you already."

She could say that again. "Why were you waiting for me, Martie?"

Another cackle, in true witch fashion, those pale eyes twinkling when she leaned forward to pinch my cheek. "I take care of them," she said, hands swiping left and right, encompassing the squat. "Heal them, tend their ills." Her joy faded. "So little left, but I give what I have." Her power glimmered, went dim. "My friends, they're gone and I don't know how to find them."

So I was right. "I want to help," I said. "I touched one of the kidnappers. He's connected to me now."

"Contagion," she said, the word faintly muffled thanks to her missing teeth. "Clever, Monday girl." Martie leaned closer then, the scent of her powerful enough I gagged just a little but refused to let her see or know. "Thieves of things," she said, "and thieves of people. First their stuff," she gestured at her carriage, "then their everything." This time she pointed at her body. "And the wards I cast, gone, shattered." Tears welled, trickled down the deep lines in her cheeks. "I can't feel them anymore." She finally covered her face in both hands, weeping softly, while my chest tightened in understanding.

Whoever was stealing from the homeless was using the theft as a chance to mark them. The kidnappings came after, though the connection to why was, as yet, to be uncovered. The fact the man who died in my house was both a thief/kidnapper and a masked witch? Led me down a road that felt a lot like the conspiracy I was considering ran deeper than trying to hurt my family.

Someone in our magical domain was conducting blood rituals to gain power, and they were using the homeless to do it.

Had my family somehow interfered with the process? Had one of us stumbled on the trail to the truth and the perpetrator decided we needed to be eliminated? That made me stop and accept my work with the police had led us here. Because it was a logical step from my uncovering of the young man who'd attacked Unk Jay-Jay leading to me ultimately discovering the fact he wasn't human if he was caught which could, I supposed, interfere with or expose those who were draining humans for magic.

"No one will listen to me," Martie said through her quiet crying. "No one, Monday girl. Will you listen?"

I nodded instantly, hugging her despite the stench. She was a person, one of my kind, a venerated elder who earned a happy and quiet retirement, not this sorry expulsion into the world to fend for herself. "I'll find them," I said. "I promise."

Martie snuffled when I let her go, wiping at her running nose with the corner of her scarf. "Thank you," she said. Met my eyes with her own piercingly focused. "But you can't, not like this."

What did she mean by that? "I'm doing my best." Nice blow to the ego there.

Instead, she touched my cheek with one fingertip, expression intent, the power she possessed blossoming against my skin in a faint flutter of butterfly wings. "No truths," she said, "until you break what holds you back."

I actually did a double take. "I don't know what you mean."

Martie dropped her hand, shrugged as though I should. "Not sure who hates you that much," she said, "but whoever it is…" her eyes widened then. "Girl, who put a curse on you?"

A.

What?

CHAPTER FIFTEEN

I'm positive if it was possible my chin would have hit the ground. "What did you say?" Even as I thought of the wards and the taint and groaned. "Did it follow me from home?"

I hadn't been speaking to Martie, not really, more to myself, but she responded as if I had, shaking her head with great seriousness.

"You carry it," she said, poking me in the chest. "Here. Shielding the best of you. And has been for a very long time."

Okay, news to me. "I had no idea," I said, faint panic rising now, my own hand rubbing my breastbone while I fought to keep my breathing even. "Any idea the source?"

She sighed then, sagging. "Not enough of it left," she said, showing me her hands again, the faint pool of her remaining power. Martie's eyes narrowed, then. "Mondays curse their own children?"

No way. "Impossible," I said. "Are you certain it's a curse?" I didn't feel anything, not a whisper. In fact, I felt exactly as I always had.

The old witch was clearly a little cracked. Could she be imagining it?

Except, when Martie touched me again, one last time, I felt it at last, the buzzing hum of the edges of the curse, surrounding me like a faint fog so amorphous and transparent it barely registered. Not strong, or unbreakable or even threatening. In fact, it registered as so subtle I could hardly believe it was there. But it was, and when I followed it within I found it, deeply embedded inside me, anchored to the power within, to the ability I had to trigger good luck in others.

Wound tight and whispering its unease through who I was.

"There," Martie said. "You see?"

I did, terror and panic now seeking control. "I don't understand." I had to talk to my family. Was this tied to what was happening?

Dear Great Mother, could I be the source of the taint?

"Its focus is ruin and death," Martie said. "I cannot break it. Only they who cast the curse have that power. You might, for a time, control it, but it has been with you for so long, has become part of you. Seek the caster to remove the curse."

She shook her head then, backed away from me while everything inside me screamed to attack the hidden controls, to scrub away what was done to me, to shatter and burn it to the ground.

I forgot why I was there, turned and ran all the way home, panting and desperate and pausing to throw up beside the dumpster on the way to the side door when my stomach finally rebelled utterly. I don't remember going inside, falling to my knees in the kitchen. I only knew I needed my family, my hearth, and that if they didn't do something to cleanse me I was going to lose my mind.

They were there, instantly, my inability to reach them earlier forgotten, the contact of our family's power renewed the moment I entered the kitchen where they sat together. I didn't speak, instead pouring out to them in image and terror what I'd been told, what was uncovered. By the time Mom, Isolde and Selene tackled me and, just past the shock of what I revealed, poured their power over me to break the curse, I was in better control of my panic. In fact, just being home, being in their company, having them circle me and take over gave me courage, buoyed my spirit, lifted my heart even as, time and again, attack after summoning after spell casting, they failed.

Utterly.

"At least I know none of you cursed me," I said in the most calm voice I'd ever heard from my own lips. I even managed a little smile while Mom sank back against the cupboards, Isolde panting, furious, Selene cross legged and weeping across from me.

"Tell us everything," my grandmother said.

Not that it helped, though Mom muttered

something that sounded like she was casting her own curse on someone under her breath, scowling at the mention of Mad Martie.

"I'll see to it," she said. "How repugnant, to make one such as her outcast. Continue."

Not just me, then. No, but the brilliant, beautiful and incredible women who I called family.

"I'm positive the kidnappings are tied to this somehow," I said, already confessing my fears about working with the police might have triggered the attack on our family. "Mirabelle should have enough to clear us, or at least raise doubt as to guilt and suspicions of conspiracy." They looked relieved enough at that. "But we still don't know so many things."

"Now that we have evidence of wrongdoing aimed at our hearth," Mom said, climbing to her feet and helping me rise, Selene doing the same for Isolde, "I can convince the Academy of Adepts to back off."

"Idiots," Isolde muttered.

"Indeed," Mom said. "In the meantime, Phoebe, my darling dear, we will find out what has happened to you and why." She hugged me against her, enveloping me with her body and her spirit, the scents of the kitchen's most delicious ingredients her personal perfume. "Whatever has been done to you will be undone."

Which meant, for the time being, I was stuck with the curse.

Suddenly exhausted, I went to bed, though it took

a long time to be able to sleep.

A visit from Selene did the trick, though, as she stroked my cheek, her power softening the edges of wakefulness, she sighed. "I know you blame yourself."

She would not make me cry. "If I'd just not used my power." Would any of this have happened?

Selene kissed my cheek. "We may not have uncovered the taint in our wards until there was no salvation for us," she said then, firmly, the Maiden assisting in my comfort, "and your curse would never have been uncovered." My sister was good at having solid points of argument against my self-recrimination. "Now, sleep, silly thing. And keep in mind, my beloved sister, you are, at times, far too kind. Not everyone deserves good luck, you know."

I almost protested. I'd never given anyone the opposite before. Found the idea repugnant. And yet. If it came down to saving my family and living with the consequences?

I knew what I'd choose.

Sleep came then, though, despite her ministrations, my dreams were haunted by nightmares of a thin, shadowed cloud chasing me and devouring me. If I jerked awake once I did it a dozen times, finally blinking, disoriented and disheveled, into the early morning light.

One bright light, Jinks lay curled up next to me, muttering to himself while he chased something in his dreams. I stroked his thick, layered fur, nuzzling the soft place between his eyebrows, smiling at his enthusiastic game despite his slumber.

I felt him wake, eyes snapping open, bright, black points full of mischief. He chattered as he rolled over on his back, inviting belly rubs, thick, plush tail thrashing in excitement.

"Where's my gift, Jinks?" Like he'd ever tell me.

He warbled something at me before leaping from the bed and dashing out of my room, a flash of red and white and black gone in an instant. It was only then the scent of cinnamon and syrup reached me, bacon a close companion, breakfast being served a floor down.

When I rose to make my bed, something tumbled to the floor and I caught myself sighing and eye rolling over the small rune stone Silas gave me, now heartily chewed by tiny fox teeth. Well, the thing hadn't worked anyway, had it? A very lucky toss aimed at my trash can ended in a slam dunk.

I could only hope it was a harbinger for how my day was about to go.

My phone buzzed as I brushed my teeth and I paused a moment to check the source of the text.

Wanted to make sure you're doing okay, Coop sent. *Thinking about you.*

I finished brushing before responding, thinking through what to say and settling on simple. *I'm okay*, I lied. Since I'd just found out my family was a target for some cruel conspiracy involving homeless humans and that I'd been carrying around a curse for years. Needed to tell him how I felt and chickened out because this was exactly the sort of thing that kept me from including a human in my life. What possible defense would he have against my kind in times of danger? Me? Yeah, he'd be better off with a girlfriend like him, as sad as that made me. I focused on the case, let that take over instead. *Have any other people gone missing?*

His reply came while I zipped up my jeans, tucking the front of my t-shirt into the waistband. *Another attack*, he sent. *This one pretty awful. Poor old woman in the hospital.*

My heart stopped. Like, no beats for so long it hurt when it started up again. Felt like forever, was probably about a half a second. Didn't matter.

I knew who the woman was, didn't I?

Mad Martie, I sent.

I could almost see his surprise through the text. *How'd you know?*

Is she okay? I hurried down the stairs, all thoughts of Mom's breakfast forgotten.

Unconscious, he sent. *And no one else is talking.*

Of course not. But they could remain silent all they wanted. I didn't need words or untruths or attempts on my family's honor. I now had proof everything was tied together. No way the attack on the old witch was a coincidence, not so soon after I'd spoken to her. Someone was watching me, or her or both. Which put me in the middle of the whole kit and kaboodle.

Now to uncover why. And who was behind it. Then, maybe we'd see if Selene was right about who deserved good luck and who didn't.

CHAPTER SIXTEEN

The house shook beneath me so suddenly I actually gasped at the feeling, the barrage of arrivals—clearly a threat if the wards reacted the way they did despite the taint that refused to be cleansed from our family power. All thoughts of Mad Martie were forgotten as I hurtled down the stairs and to the kitchen where, stunned into stillness, I stared at the assembly of six stern-faced and black robed inquisitors standing in the sunny space. While Mom's favorite domain was large under normal conditions, having so many people uncomfortably crowded into the kitchen, a few with chagrin on their faces as they brushed flour from their persons and one batted at a puff of smoke where her cloak had come too close to the open flame on the gas stove, made the bright and white room feel oppressive.

Served the inquisitor right, singing herself, barging in here like that. Would have been amusing if the situation wasn't so serious.

Silas appeared a moment later and, for reasons unknown, brought Elias with him. I dodged the younger Gael when he instantly circled the crowd, heading my way, tucking in behind Selene to avoid contact. I didn't need his help and certainly wasn't interested in whatever he thought his attention would gain him, thanks.

Except, as the head inquisitor unfurled a parchment—the official document sparking in red to match the interior of his cloak—Elias made it to my side as if by magic while the inquisitor spoke.

"By the word of law of the Academy of Adepts," he said in a booming voice that was really freaking unnecessary, thanks, "we hereby formally accuse the witches Monday of blood ritual magic and shall begin our official investigation forthwith."

Now, I wasn't one to speak up typically. That was my mother's job, one she was very good at. Despite that truth, I found myself pushing past Selene and confronting the tall, skinny inquisitor with anger making my heart pound.

"So the report presented to you by Mirabelle Whitehall means nothing?" He glared down at me while I planted my fists on my hips, shaking with the need to smack him for his arrogance. Where this sudden surge of bravery came from I had no idea, except that this was my family we were talking about and I was not going down without a fight.

"Insufficient as deemed by the Academy of Adepts," he said in the snobbiest tone I'd ever heard while looking down at me from his superior height and apparent assumed station while my power surged inside me.

Wanting *out*.

"Despite the fact," I wasn't backing down, astonishing myself and, from the faint grin on Isolde's face, my grandmother, "there is evidence someone disguised one of us as a human? And the very same magic user," I turned to look each of the other five inquisitors in the face before turning back to him, "who is tied to the kidnappings of homeless humans, likely the very source of the blood rituals you claim we're part of?"

That raised a few gasps of surprise, though the head inquisitor didn't seem all that concerned. His fellows might, for the most part, have had a shift in attitude—many now with doubt and worry on their faces—but he remained stoically locked into idiocy.

"All will be revealed during the investigation." He snapped the parchment shut, the sheet rolling back into its curve with a whoosh of air.

"This is an outrage." Silas spoke up, but it was Mom who stepped forward, staring the tall inquisitor down.

"The Monday hearth has done nothing wrong," she said, the steady and confident Mother showing in her. "We welcome your investigation, Inquisitor Fallview." Mom knew this jerkface? From the tightening of his already thin lips and the way he seemed to view her with distaste, they had to have history. So, was this a personal vendetta? Just what we needed. Did I need to add him to the suspect list? Yup, too much time at the police department, and yet, hard not to consider that an option. "We are assured, I assume, of unbiased treatment?" There was just enough sarcasm in her voice I knew I'd guessed right.

"You will be questioned and your guilt decided," he snapped, his opinion already cemented, and everyone in the room knew it.

Just freaking great.

I backed off as the inquisitors separated my family, taking Selene out of the room, trying to escort Isolde by a hand on her arm which she rejected in her most haughty and disdainful fashion that had the young female inquisitor almost apologizing. Mom swept from the kitchen like the queen she was, Fallview on her heels, Silas following while I was ignored by the gathering.

So, they were only here for the threesome that was the wonderworking of the Maiden, Mother and Crone. Instantly suspect and raised my hackles. Now convinced of a conspiracy, I knew I had to find proof, no matter what it took, and uncover who was trying to take out my family.

When I turned to leave, I almost ran headlong into Elias Gael who, it seemed, had been waiting behind me for a moment alone. He caught me with both hands, staring down at me with those icy blue eyes, trying a smile that only triggered my dislike. The physical contact gave me the willies, goosebumps rising. Again with the familiarity of him, as odd feeling as it had been from the night we met. Why did he feel like I'd known him forever? Couldn't be natural and, when I pulled free, a few faint golden sparks from his hands told me he'd tried magic on me.

More than enough reason to doubt his intentions and confirm my own suspicions he had motives I simply wasn't interested in.

"My uncle will take care of everything," he said like he really believed it.

"My family," I shot back, "is innocent and the truth will out. Now, if you'll excuse me." I tried to walk past him, felt his hand on my arm again. That same tingle of rejection from my own magic whispered he hadn't let up on the influencing me with power department. Something he'd regret if he tried it again.

"I hope so," he said. "For your sake."

While his words and attitude, that sad smile, those wide eyes, the sympathy in his voice all bespoke an attempt at comfort and kindness, everything in me rejected him so powerfully I actually wiped at my arm where he'd touched me, where the yellow flickers of magic danced a moment between us.

He frowned, just a flash of one, just for a moment, but enough it showed in his eyes. The truth of him, the manipulation he attempted, a weak and pathetic attempt. Did he think me that out of touch with my own magic he could just bulldoze me over and play the fake protector? Clearly, that was the case.

Way to underestimate me, jackass.

"Elias." Silas poked his nose into the kitchen, looking back and forth between us. Was that a moment of irritation? Was the uncle as frustrated and annoyed by the nephew as I was? "To me."

The younger Gael left me with a reluctant flash of rebellion in his icy eyes, and for the first time, I caught a real glimpse of the man inside. So pretty, wasn't he, his shell that perfect form of strength and facial features and height. All hiding a rotten soul within.

Silas waited for Elias to leave before shrugging to me, his own face sad. "I'm so sorry, my dear," he said. "I'll do what I can."

"Thank you," I said. Fell silent. Waited for him to leave. Which he did, finally, clearly at a loss for words.

Which was fine by me. I was tired of talking.

Time for doing.

I snuck out of the house, and though no one seemed inclined to stop me, I still had an uncomfortable moment at the side door when one of the inquisitors decided to block the exit.

Maybe I should have felt badly for what I did next, but I found it hard to muster any kind of regret for the actions I took. After all, the policing arm of the Academy of Adepts knew they were here under false pretenses so if they decided to continue the farce, they were fair game.

At least, that was the excuse I clung to while

gritting my teeth, hearing Selene's voice in my head, and approached him on foot while nudging him just the barest bit with bad luck.

Relieved I didn't burst instantly into flames for the imagined transgression against my own power. Actually felt the boost in my energy when my magic softly shooed him into a new path in an effortless shuffle that left me sighing softly that the magic inside me, at least, had zero qualms acting in that manner.

I wasn't sure what might happen since I was usually the one suffering from the effects of my ability, I was delighted when he was summoned in a loud voice by Inquisitor Fallview just as I rounded the corner toward the door.

His bad luck paired with a dose of good on my side and I was free, grabbing my coat and boots on the way by, shivering in the cold while I dressed once outside just in case.

It had only been a nudge, so he might notice a bit of a downward spiral the next twenty-four hours, but nothing that would make my interference stand out. I hoped. As for my reversal of fortunes, I'd take all the luck I could get.

Hard not to feel a little guilty for leaving my family to deal with the inquisitors, huddling inside my coat and hat, mittened hands stuffed in my pockets, kicking at snow with my boots while I tried to think of what to do next. I paused at the corner, thinking things through. While human evidence might not be the answer, what Morales and Sallow dug up could help guide me in the right direction. I considered calling Coop, but I really didn't want to include him in the mess any further.

Step one, however, was closer than I thought. I retraced my steps to the shantytown where I'd spoken to Mad Martie. If she had been attacked by the same man I'd come in contact with, there should be evidence of his presence.

The moment the empty lot was in sight, I saw them, the floating golden sparks the contagion spell left behind. I was almost bouncing as I rushed to Martie's cardboard house, the collection of wisps leading to her space and then out the back, where they gathered near the street before thinning out.

He'd been here, beat the poor old witch unconscious, but left her behind. Likely because she was one of us. He had to be, too. Something I hadn't thought of before, not until that moment. Luck or my mind finally catching up with me? Whatever the case, I whispered a spell of binding, feeling the power of the kidnapper snap into focus, made all the easier thanks to the original contact.

I followed the floating sparks, whispering to them inside the binding. Another simple incantation that required little power, but delivered as I stepped onto the next street and watched the wafting parade of golden particles dancing their dreamy residue in a perfect trail to follow.

I wasn't surprised they led me back to the seemingly abandoned building, nor that they pooled once again outside. This time, however, I realized why it was they seemed to go nowhere from there.

Hadn't thought to check if the building was warded, had I? Because I had no idea the kidnapper was one of us. But, with that information in hand and the energized connection boosting the signal? Impossible to miss the wall of protection encircling the building.

My luck held, apparently, because the moment I stopped to examine the wards, barely breathing my own power across them, the sort of echo location thrumming against the barrier, a van pulled up. Which sent me tucking around the corner, peeking out enough to see but, hopefully with the luck I had humming around me, not be seen.

Two men got out.

And headed inside.

This time, however, they weren't wearing masks and while I didn't know the taller driver, the other was oh, so familiar when he paused at the door and looked back, like he sensed someone was watching him.

Because I was. And Elias Gael had a lot of explaining to do.

CHAPTER SEVENTEEN

Of course it was him. I almost kicked myself for not making the connection earlier. The familiarity of him wasn't from his power trying to subvert mine, the gold sparks when he touched me triggered by the law of contagion. I hadn't been using my inner sight on him, however, so I'd only caught a few. If I'd just thought to examine him more closely, I could have exposed him at the house.

The two disappeared inside the building, wards sealing around them. Which put me at an impasse. I could go inside, break past the protections, but alert them in the process. Mind you, I did have enhanced luck on my side at the moment, but I wasn't counting on that to keep me safe from two magic users who clearly didn't care who they hurt. Besides, I had very little by way of battle magic, had never tested well in offensive magicks. All I really had were small castings, little bits and pieces of spell work most of our kind could access. Sketching memories didn't count, as far as I could tell.

That left my synchromysticism. I couldn't help but think about the curse I carried, shivering inside my jacket, nothing to do with the cold. Was I capable of more? So hard to know past the shadowy veil that I now felt almost continually since Martie uncovered it for me. The need to take a shower would do nothing to cleanse it, however, and I could do nothing about it anyway until I found out who cast it in the first place. That meant pulling up my big witch bloomers and focusing on what I could do, not what I couldn't.

Even as the front door opened again and Elias exited, now dressed in a hoody and jacket, the hood pulled up, sneakers and jeans that innocuous uniform I was now so familiar with. Especially when he pulled a ski mask out of his pocket while striding across the street.

Heading my way.

I meeped just a bit when I made the connection I really should hide or something and had enough luck to duck into a half-open doorway. He didn't even glance my way, hurrying back the way I'd come. For the shantytown and the residents there?

Over my cold and frozen body.

It felt weird to trail him, unnatural to follow, like I found myself in some kind of bad Hollywood TV show where the idiot heroine decided to play private eye and ended up having to be saved by the handsome hero. Except, this idiot heroine was on her own and it was highly unlikely—a stretch even for the good luck I'd created—I'd have anyone ride to my rescue.

That meant, whatever was going to happen, whatever I was going to do to make Elias admit what he'd been up to, it was all up to me.

I must have discarded half a dozen plans of action—including a ridiculous and desperate fantasy involving roundhouse kicking him into submission though I had zero experience with martial arts but was oddly satisfying and had me grinning—by the time he turned the last corner and paused to observe the shanty. I stopped myself, positive he was going to find me, spot me, a bundle of nerves and excitement, if I was going to be honest, while all thoughts of what I might do next vanished in a wash of *what the heck was I thinking, anyway.*

Even as a small woman in a tattered coat emerged from her cardboard shack and ducked behind it.

Elias was moving so suddenly I had to run to catch up, was donning the ski mask as he passed the sidewalk to the empty lot. Part of me had to admire in a breathless kind of *holy crap* the sheer audacity of his full-daylight plan of attack. When he followed the woman, face shielded but identity impossible to hide from me, disappearing behind the pile of boxes, I sped up, not thinking or planning or even breathing as I plunged into the shadows after him.

And stumbled over him dragging the woman to the ground, one hand over her mouth to silence her screams and the other around her throat.

Time stood still and the only thing that flashed through my mind propelled me to act. Selene, stroking my hair back from my face, lying on my bed, just last night.

Not everyone deserves good luck.

We were already connected, Elias and myself. It was simple enough to lunge forward and touch him, strengthen the moment, cinch in the bond, past his personal protections he clearly hadn't expected to need, as his head turned and those blue eyes stared, wide and shocked, into mine.

At the exact moment I spoke. "Bad boy," I whispered, digging deep, following the darkest path, the deepest fall into despair and destruction, pushing his entire being sideways into the darkness I saw for him. For the first time, I embraced what I could do fully, without restriction and, in that moment, felt everything I was fall away.

No emotion or judgement, zero regret and guilt, no thought for the outcome crossed my mind as the power within me shifted his entire life from the blessed path he'd been walking—powered, clearly, by blood ritual magic—to the ruin that was now his fate.

How remarkable to accept what I could do. I'd always held it in check, no idea just how much of it was truly available to me. My power burbled, remorseless in the surge of power that passed between us. I almost pulled back at the last moment, a part of me regaining myself, fighting the purity of choice, while the uncomfortable edge of the curse made itself known, capping off the access I'd just learned I had.

It wanted me to stop. Put itself between me and Elias. And only then did I realize why.

The surge that recognized him revealed its truth and I understood, even past the contagion spell, the binding, that he felt so familiar for a reason.

All the way to the curse I carried.

He'd had a chance at my pity, but lost it when the curse wailed its revelation. Which only made me push harder. Unleashing the kind of energy I'd never had the need—or, frankly, the courage—to use before.

The worst luck ever latched onto Elias Gael and embedded itself so deeply inside him I knew this was no twenty-four hour stint. He'd carry the repercussions of my attack for the rest of his life.

Wasn't sorry.

Elias collapsed clutching his head, black passing over those icy eyes, hands scrabbling to pull free the ski mask covering his face. The woman he'd attacked ran, leaving me there with him, but I didn't mind.

Could barely muster a whisper of anything past the giant surge of *HECKEN YESSAH* that lifted me in a wave of such delicious vibration I laughed out loud.

Dear. Great. Mother.

Yes.

But, wait.

Answers were important and I would not let death take him just yet.

The curse lingered between us, the connections I'd made, enough I felt the swelling aneurysm growing in his brain, saw the imminent end it would mean, and pivoted.

Had no idea I could, acted on impulse. Guided him away from that ultimate end while he screamed in agony, down a different path, hauling his power and his fate, kicking and shrieking, to the next worse thing. Then the next, when death was again his end, until I jerked him, unable to fight me further, into a satisfying thread of destiny that made me smile.

I hoped he saw that expression, because it satisfied me to no end to see what awaited him.

"You're welcome," I said. "I could have let you die. Instead, enjoy where your evil is taking you." I turned my power's back on him at last, the sight of the cell he would occupy the rest of his life—yes, I could have let him burn, but this was way better—devolving him into madness before too long.

Only then did my power let him go.

Elias sobbed, hunched over on his knees, curling protectively around himself while I stood over him and felt my will return, my emotions kick-starting into who I'd been raised to be while my power, humming happily, retreated to simmer in its delight at being let loose at last.

Okay, so a bit of guilt. How about a lot?

"You're kidnapping homeless humans for blood rituals." I let that sink into him a moment while he struggled to sit up, still weeping, face contorted into horror and despair.

"What did you do to me?" He rocked where he crouched, a broken and terrified animal, no longer handsome, no longer a danger to me or anyone. I'd seen to that.

No guilt, Phoebe.

"I gave you the fate you deserve," I said, "for what you've done. I just don't get why. Why steal from them first?"

Elias shuddered, staring at his hands, then up at me, pale, so pale. "We had to be sure they were free of magic," he said. "Some humans have traces inside them. Stealing their stuff first made it easy to check, and humanity's trash rarely report to the police." Was he trying to piss me off further? "If they passed, we took them." The law of contagion at work again, huh? Clever and awful at the same time.

"Who are you working with?" Keep talking, buster. "Because there's no way you came up with this yourself." Oh, a horrible, truly awful, thought crossed my mind then, but my phone rang, pulling me out of the panicked understanding, drawing me instead to answer.

"Phoebe," Mirabelle said. "I found something inside the body." She sounded excited, happy. "It's the same taint as your wards. I told the inquisitors, and they admitted they found the same thing in the house." Ah, happy luck. "I thought you'd want to know, your family has been cleared."

"Thank you," I said, that fluttering despair in the back of my throat making it hard to speak. "Can you tell me what it is?"

"I sent you a photo," she said. "I'm sorry, Phoebe. Really sorry. I'll never doubt your family again." She hung up then, my phone vibrating with the arrival of the image.

I didn't have to look at it, already knew what I'd see.

Still checked because sometimes watching a train wreck is the only option.

And knew, didn't I? Knew exactly who led the young druid down this path. The same person who created the curse, tied it to Elias, because it was clear now that I had contact with it, with him, my sparkling luck shedding light where only shadows had been, that Elias was the keystone, but not the source.

He'd been used to anchor the curse to me, tied into another magic user. To hide it from me, so the source remained undetectable. That was the only explanation that made sense. The fact Elias had finally come into my life could only mean one thing.

The curse, reinforced over and over again, across the years, through the guise of trying to help me with the repercussions of my power, only with the opposite intent had now come to some kind of fruition and the caster was ready to act. Why else would my old family friend expose me to what he'd done?

Didn't matter, not really. The blow of the betrayal was enough to keep my attention for the moment. While I decided to do something about it.

CHAPTER EIGHTEEN

Elias looked up at me then, blue eyes no longer bright, rather a dulled out gray now. The creep had used magic to enhance his features, his face lacking that glowing handsomeness he'd worn, settling into plain and rather ordinary. Which made me wonder. About others in the Academy of Adepts and just how deeply this whole mess ran.

No time for that, not when Elias was speaking.

"He forced me to," he said, deep voice now a whining irritation, a mosquito's humming in my ear only worthy of swatting. "When I was a boy, he forced me to carry your curse."

"Why?" I'd known Silas my whole life. He was a dedicated and kindly friend to my family. Except, apparently, he wasn't.

"Your power." Elias curved inward on himself again, hugging his arms around his torso, still weeping. "Something to do with your birth. He never said, only that you weren't meant to be. He said the only way to control you was to make sure your magic was tied down, but you couldn't know, not until he was ready to act. So he had to carry the curse for you." His sobbing ended suddenly, eyes slitted, cornered beast ready to attack. "He said he would reward me, but he lied." Sorry, no sympathy here. "He's always hated you," he said, "and your family." Elias spit on the ground, though when he did his lower lip cracked in the cold, blood trickling from the tear, the wad hitting his knee instead of the pavement. Bad luck in action. "When he found out you were investigating the missing homeless, sketching for the police, he knew it was only a matter of time before you uncovered the truth. He'd always kept me away from you, but when he chose to make his move on your family, it was time for us to meet."

"He thought the familiar power would connect us and distract me," I said. Made sense.

"More than that," Elias said. "He planned let go of the anchor and release the full curse. Free me. Except it backfired." His face contorted. "I don't know why."

I did. "Bad luck," I said. And laughed.

Before reaching out to Mom.

Contemplated waiting for the inquisitors like she asked.

Decided to trust my luck—that bright and shining luck burning inside me that surely meant nothing could go wrong—because one way or another, Silas would get what was coming to him.

I felt them arrive when I was crossing the street, ignored their presence and continued on as if floating on air. Amazing how great I felt despite everything, how I caught the perfect gap in the traffic, that the sidewalk had just been scraped and salted, that the sun came out and warmed up the day. Even how pedestrians just seemed to melt out of my path, the way I caught every green light at the exact moment I needed it. Subtle things, and mere cast off from the truly epic awesomeness I felt bubbling inside of me.

Today, if I so chose, I could accomplish anything.

The wards of the abandoned building were no match for my power, shimmering as I passed them, naturally recognizing the curse I still carried and accepting me as Elias or, at least, a part of the power that created it. I could get used to this, really, while I didn't even pause at the doorway, treading on soft boots through the dusty front of the open space, the sound of voices up ahead drawing me on.

Droning voices, one of them familiar enough I knew everything I'd uncovered was true, the other inconsequential.

A set of stairs at the back of the building carried me down into the dark, toward the voice I knew so well. While power thrummed around me, still unconcerned, wasn't it, thanks to luck and the fact he'd cursed me when I was a child.

I could have called on Mom and Isolde, Selene and Mirabelle. Asked the Academy of Adepts to help me, requested inquisitors to save the day. Absolutely within my rights and seeing as Elias was in their custody, my family cleared, and the truth of the darkness I approached now impossible to hide, I could have stepped back and let justice prevail.

Except, I had no idea, did I, just how deep the rot ran and, in this enhanced state of excellent luck I'd created for myself, I was just the person to ensure Silas Gael got what was coming to him.

Mom, I sent as I touched down on the basement floor, flickering firelight up ahead luring me as much as the droning of the druid's deep voice. *Send inquisitors here.* I let her feel where I was. *In about ten minutes.*

Phoebe, sweetheart, she sent. Paused as she sampled my power through our connection. Laughed. *Ten minutes.*

I truly loved my mother.

A door at the far end of the corridor I found myself in stood partly open, the flame's flickering and Silas's words coming from within. I didn't stop, letting momentum carry me into the small room, though I finally paused, the knowing of what he was doing no real preparation for the actual truth.

A young man, his body dirty and hair matted, had been fixed to a stone altar, his hands and feet bound with power, the runes of druid earth magic linking him to the dull, gray rock as though he was part of it. He fought soundlessly, those same runes covering his gaping mouth, the scream trapped behind the power that held him written across his scarlet face, in his bulging eyes, naked body but for a loincloth tied around his waist writhing as magic carved slow, circular trails and etched precise, burning lines into his flesh.

I couldn't look up for the longest time, my entire being taking in the horrible unfolding of the blood ritual. Only when the tall, black robed spell caster stepped around the cursed shrine did I glance away, motion taking my attention as a mercy.

Silas hadn't noticed me yet, still droned his powerful call, the visible siphoning of the young man's essence climbing from the smoking etchings, inhaled into the druid's nostrils and past his lips while he intoned his spell. Only my luck kept me safe, I was sure of that, because now that I had broken free of the horrible sight before me, I realized I'd come to a halt one pace behind the tall, young man Silas recruited, the one I'd seen driving the van and at Elias's side.

My power demanded action and, before the druid could finish, I would end this. Inhaled slowly, let the synchromysticism take over. Felt it rush over the young man beside me, his path to darkness so clear I only had to tip him over into it, forget him, he was toast. While the bulk of the power hit Silas Gael full in the chest.

Nothing happened. Wait, what? The attack collapsed in a bitter sigh of failure when the old druid looked up and met my eyes.

"Phoebe," he said as though he'd been expecting me, the sizzling magical runes pausing in their advancement, the young man on the slab falling still as the pain stopped for the moment. "How remarkable. I hadn't thought you could make it this far. I should never have trusted Elias to deal with you." He gestured at me, the door slamming shut in my wake. Why hadn't it worked? I swallowed, realizing I'd likely just stepped into the fire with the kind of arrogance I hadn't earned when he spoke again, soft smile no longer the kind one I remembered, but tainted.

By the curse he built for me.

"You have no idea the time I've spent on you," he said, so casual, so confident, hands waving over the young man before him. At least I didn't have the other druid to worry about. He'd fallen to the floor, gibbering at his hands like he'd never seen them before. The path I'd sent him down led to madness and I would not relent. Neither, it seemed, would Silas. "All the power I put into making sure you never, ever had access to what lives inside you."

The curse, the hesitation I had using my power. All from Silas? I almost lost it, reined in my anger, my fury, wanting to weep and scream while the luck that held me in its amazing embrace kept me together. "Afraid of me or something?" I couldn't stand still any longer, slowly circled the makeshift altar, needing at least some outlet for the rage inside me. Rage aimed at him that had nowhere to go. "You should be."

Silas chuckled, shook his head. "As long as the curse I created exists, your power remains contained." Was that a frown on his face, a moment of confusion. "What have you done to Elias?"

Didn't see that coming, did he? "Only set him on the path he deserved," I said, that moment of bravado fed by Silas's confusion and anger. "Any last words before I do the same to you?"

Meaningless, because I'd already thrown everything I had at him. Failed.

The curse. How could I break it?

Silas's expression stilled. "You've called the inquisitors," he said. Shrugged. "No matter. They will arrive and discover I've caught you at your dark work. That you are the source of the Monday taint. And, when you are gone, I will find a new way to control the wonderworking your family has hoarded all these centuries."

As if it would ever answer to him. "All those times you said you were trying to help me," I shot at him, coming to a halt at the head of the altar, the young homeless man's eyes turned up to me with hope and terror. "You were reinforcing the curse."

"Indeed." Silas sounded bored by the conversation. "That fool, Niall Shermer, wasn't supposed to enter the house. He was merely meant to leave the new runestone at the door for you to find. Instead, he was caught in the very wards I'd been tainting to bring you low." He sighed then, rubbed at his tall forehead with one long-fingered hand. "So hard to find good help these days. Even my own nephew is a terrible disappointment." Silas's smile had a decidedly evil twist to it. How had I missed his duplicity? The curse, of course. "Though, I suppose it was your ill luck that led to Shermer's death. Did you know your arrival coincided with his?"

I hadn't, though the soft punch of something I'd felt when I'd landed reminded me Silas had to be right. That weird impact I'd felt when I'd passed the wards and touched down on the roof triggered the ward's protection of me and, in doing so, ended the young man's life. But only because he bore me and the family ill will. Bad luck for both of us. "You took his spirit." It was the only explanation for where it had gone.

"Naturally," Silas said. "I owned him. And so, his spirit came to me the instant of his death." He sighed, as though burdened by the young man's death instead of regretful. "You know, I should thank you for freeing me of the task that has been caring for my dead sister's child once and for all." He really was a horrible person and I had some serious soul-searching to do because I'd believed otherwise all this time.

My badguydar was busted, apparently, if I didn't blame the curse.

"You're welcome," I said. "Too bad your plan failed and you're about to be arrested for blood ritual magic and murder. No one will believe this is me. Not in the state of luck I'm carrying." So there.

Silas's lack of concern registered, even through my adrenaline rush.

"We shall see," he said. "Though perhaps you overestimate the regard in which your family is held and underestimate the power I wield. No matter." He inhaled and whispered over the young man, the fire inside the etching starting up again. "I'll be done here momentarily, and then we will see what the curse I've nurtured for so long can really do."

"What do you mean?" Okay, time to panic.

Silas paused, thick brows arching. "You really think I would invest all this time into you, into having what I've always wanted, only to fail?" He tsked softly. "The curse you bear feeds the wards your family built so many years ago and has for as long as I have controlled you. When the time comes, I will simply drain the wonderworking from your family through you and that, my dear, will be the end of the Monday witches."

Just like that. So casual, so callous.

And there was nothing I could do about it.

Or was there?

I reached for Mom, couldn't find her. Even as connections clicked inside my head and the only option I had left made me wince before acting.

Drawing into me the power I'd dreaded my whole life, only so very recently learned to embrace, knowing I was about to have a very, very bad day. Not caring if it worked and saved my family.

Because Silas's plan had failed, hadn't it? Thanks to my bad luck.

Which was why, as he finished his ritual, ignoring me, choosing to see me as a means to an end, I focused completely on him. On the curse tying us together, the link visible now, only because I knew it was there. Jerked free the end still embedded in Elias on the street above, took it firmly in my magical grasp, felt the end snap back where it belonged all along. To Silas. While he shuddered, gaped at me. Even as I sent him, in a giant push down a sparkly path I drew close to us both, down the very best and shiniest and brightest string of happy happenstance and BEST LUCK EVER I could muster.

There was a reason trying to give him bad luck didn't work. The same reason the opposite sent him, screaming in agony, to his knees. The anchor of the curse had a rebound like a snapping rubber band, only with a lifetime of dark and horrible magic behind it. His plan to pull stakes and give me the full brunt of whatever it was he'd created? Did the reverse to him, thanks to the coming together of all that amazing luck.

While my entire being shimmered and sang as he howled his denial at being forced to accept the lifetime of pending awful I was supposed to bear when the curse sprang back to its maker.

Take that, asshat.

CHAPTER NINETEEN

I squinted at the fresh sketch I'd just created, pondering the paint colors I wanted to use to bring the entwined figures to life. I had the perfect canvas waiting, a four-foot vertical that would house the male and female abstract in the most amazing way.

Nice to focus on my art for a while, now that my world had (mostly) gone back to normal. Right down to the scent of Christmas Eve dinner floating through my door, the summons a clear message from my mother the feast was almost ready.

Hard to believe, in a way, two days had passed since Silas's collapse, since the inquisitors arrived, Fallview still looking down his nose at me but more than willing to take the druid and his protégé into custody. I'd made myself scarce while they rescued the poor homeless man, knowing his memories would be altered enough to ensure he never shared what really happened in the basement of the abandoned building.

Or, if he did, no one would believe him anyway.

I closed my sketchbook, tucking my pencils into the case Selene gave me years ago, her huge, smiling face on the outside meant as a joke but something that always made me grin. A long stretch when I stood shook off the kinks, though the lingering touch of shadow flickered in my peripheral vision, taking the enjoyment out of the moment.

Despite Silas's capture and pending sentencing, the curse remained. Maybe, when they burned him, I'd finally be free, but I wasn't counting on it. Whatever he'd done to me, it was now clear the recoil I'd created in my attack had severed it from his influence. In doing so, I'd cut him off while claiming the thing as my own.

Which meant, I was now the proud owner of my very own curse that refused to go away no matter what I did.

Never mind. I'd find the answer. And clear myself of his influence—and the effect the curse had on my power—forever.

Grim thoughts after such a victory.

As was Selene's quiet admission Jericho Richmond was no longer interested.

"He was never worthy of a Monday," she'd told me the previous night, sniffing in fake arrogance before shrugging with a sad look in her eyes. "He is very pretty, though."

If false accusations was all it took for him to drop my amazing, gorgeous and talented sister? I figured she dodged a bullet, thanks.

I tucked my phone into my back pocket, thinking about Mirabelle Whitehall. She'd called this morning, not to talk about the now finalized case, to my surprise, but just to chat. It had been so long since I'd had one of our kind as a friend, I wasn't sure how to take it, but I hung up from the short conversation smiling, so I guess I didn't do too badly.

"Have a great Christmas," she said. "See you soon?"

That sounded like a great idea.

Morales called me, to my surprise, to tell me the case had been wrapped up. Someone decided Elias Gael would pay for his uncle's plan in the human world, since someone had to.

"Turns out the dead guy was the ring leader and this Gael kid had a beef," Morales said. "ME says they fought while robbing your place. They fought and the other kid, Shermer, fell, hit his head, and Gael just took off."

Of course, I knew better, that Mirabelle had altered the physical evidence, and happily accepted Morales's sequence of events.

"See you in the new year," she'd said, before hanging up.

Guess I was still working for the police department. Just my luck.

Even better news had come from Coop, a quick text fired off shortly after I hung up from Mirabelle.

Martie woke up, he sent. *She's going to be okay.*

She certainly was. Because when I told Mom the

witch had come out of her unconscious state, it was to the Mother's firm hug and reassurance.

"She will have a hearth again," she said. "Already in the works, Phoebe. Thanks to you."

Well. Good luck lingered, I guess.

Which made me wonder about my power, something I'd been doing a lot of the last two days. While the excessive good luck vanished, cancelled out when I broke Silas's attempt to control me, it wasn't lost on me he'd seemed to think my magic was important. Worth examining more closely. I'd always been hesitant to do so, considering the consequences. But, if I could understand it better, could I find a way to break the last of the curse, no longer connected to the druid, at least, but a revenant scrap of magic that lurked inside me, like a hideous doppelganger I couldn't shake?

Worth looking into.

I knew Mom, Isolde and Selene were more than happy to help. Time to take them up on their offer, if only as a rebellion against the constant pressure I only now knew I lived under, Silas's controls gone and leaving me sad for what I'd missed out on.

No more, Phoebe Monday.

Selene sang as she passed my door, heading downstairs to the kitchen, matching, as I entered the hall, the sound of Mom's voice coming up toward her. I stood there in the quiet upstairs for a moment, hearing them finish their harmony and laugh together under my feet, inhaling the delicious scent of dinner waiting below.

While Isolde, clearly ahead of my sister, yelled at the two of them to bring her more chocolate.

My family. How did I get to be so lucky? Oh, yeah. Right.

Awesome.

I almost missed Jinks, the brat, as he slipped past me and ducked into my room. The only reason I turned back? The shining something he had in his jaws. Sneaking suspicions confirmed when I found him curled up on my bed, gnawing on the silver wrapping.

"Finally," I said.

He grinned at me, tail thrashing while I retrieved Coop's present, ruffling the silly fox's ears. Jinks chattered, and I swear he was laughing at me, resting his head on my lap, shining eyes looking up at me with the kind of false innocence that cancelled out any chance I could stay mad at him.

"Bad fox," I said. Stroked the soft fur between his ears, the velvet of those black peaks. "Silly Jinks. Jealous?"

His tail thumped once before he fell still again.

I almost waited. Was going to put the small box—the paper now worse for wear and minus the bow—under the tree for tomorrow. Instead, hands trembling just a little, I peeled the silver foil away, setting it between the fox's paws. He ignored it, watching with intent while I stared down at the black velvet square in my hands.

Contemplated just returning the gift to Coop, writing off this whatever it was between us once and for all. Flipped open the top with a soft creak of hinges.

And gasped at the beautiful silver moon necklace nestled inside.

The chain felt far too delicate in my hands as I lifted it free of the box, giving that to Jinks, too. He stared with wide eyes, and I knew, given the chance, the little thief would make off with my gift for real. Rather than provide such an opportunity, I fastened the clasp around my neck, breathing a soft sealing spell to safeguard the catch until I released it, and stood to check the fall of the pendant in the mirror of my wardrobe.

The crescent curve sat perfectly in the hallow of my throat and I found I had to clear it with a soft cough, grinning at the sparkling gift while my eyes burned with tears I wasn't expecting.

So thoughtful, that gift. I'd been trying to imagine what it would be like. Actually following through on going to his suburban human house for his family party, having him as a boyfriend, a partner. I knew what a terrible idea that could turn into. Sure, some witches chose normal mates, but usually from those who already understood who we were, those few who we made part of our world. And never a Monday.

Coop had no idea what he had been hoping to get himself into.

As a final thought, before I could stop myself, I whispered one last spell. The law of contagion, once used as a way to track a thief, now tied me to the spirit that was Cooper Hudson. A silly little incantation, but one I hugged myself over once it was done.

Decision made. Surely the whole Elias being a thief thing would clear up any concern he might have I had feelings for the young druid. And, perhaps, give me the chance I needed to tell Coop how I really felt.

Right after I figured it out myself.

As for the handsome cop, he'd clearly already decided he wanted to be with me. So there wasn't any harm in it, right? Except, I knew how powerful silver was, my element, and that clearing the connection when—or if—I so chose would take a lot of effort on my part.

Might break my heart.

Oh well. Weren't they made to be broken?

With my lovely gift glistening around my neck, I grinned at my reflection before scooping up Jinks and heading down to dinner.

Looking for more Phoebe Monday? Have no fear, book two is here! Find **Death Warmed Over** at all fine retailers.

AUTHOR NOTES

My darling reader:

I hope you enjoyed this first in Phoebe Monday's series. She's just one of two new voices I'm exploring right now, and I'm adoring her. While she's younger than I've been writing lately, returning to a world of magic while mixing in murder feels not only right, but where I'm happiest, I think.

So look for more Phoebe Monday coming soon!

Meanwhile, check out the first chapter of book one my brand-new series, **Whitewitch Island Paranormal Cozies.** *Dead Even*. I can't wait for you to meet Georgia Drake!

And, as an extra treat, chapter one of *Social Medium*, book one of the **Alice Moore Paranormal Cozies**. Both first in series are FREE right now!

Best,
Patti

ABOUT THE AUTHOR

Everything you need to know about me is in this one statement: I've wanted to be a writer since I was a little girl, and now I'm doing it. How cool is that, being able to follow your dream and make it reality? I've tried everything from university to college, graduating the second with a journalism diploma (I sucked at telling real stories), am an enthusiastic member of an all-girl improv troupe, Side Hustle (if you've never tried it, I highly recommend making things up as you go along as often as possible) and I get to teach and perform with an amazing group of women I adore.

I've even been in a Celtic girl band (some of our stuff is on YouTube!) and was an independent film maker (go check out the Lovely Witches Club at https://www.lovelywitchesclub.com). My life has been one creative thing after another—all leading me here, to writing books for a living.

Now with multiple series in happy publication, I live on beautiful and magical Prince Edward Island (I know you've heard of Anne of Green Gables) with my multitude of pets.

I love-love-love hearing from you! You can reach me (and I promise I'll message back) at patti@pattilarsen.com. And if you're eager for your next dose of Patti Larsen books (usually about one release a month) come join my mailing list! All the best up and coming, giveaways, contests and, of